ROCK THE CHARDONNAY

STEAMY ROCKSTAR ROMANCE

NATALIE CROSS

Trigger Warnings

Toxic Mom Drama
    Sibling Infighting
    Chemistry Puns
    Using Sex as a Coping Mechanism
    This is a steamy romance, so there's explicit language, dirty talking, and explicit love scenes, with a little dose of praise kink.
    Don't we all secretly want to be good girls?

CHAPTER 1

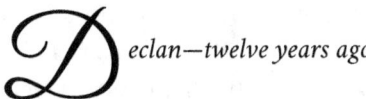 *eclan—twelve years ago*

IF MY EYEBALLS actually burst into flames, will that excuse me from the organic chemistry midterm?

I glare at my laptop screen while playing with my plastic ball-and-stick model of the chemical compound for banana ester. Seven carbons, fourteen hydrogens, and one—no, damn it—two oxygens. I pick up another of the large blue balls that I'm using to simulate oxygen and attach it to my model.

A girlish laugh filters down the stairs of my family's otherwise silent house. Blue balls. That's not something my brother, Ciaran, ever has to worry about. Not that he worries about grades, either. Or anything, really, apart from girls and hockey.

My stomach curdles. Too much hydrochloric acid, brought on by too many sleepless nights cramming for midterms and too many glasses of my family vineyard's red blend. I know I shouldn't combine the two. I'm supposed to be smarter than that.

Footsteps sound in the upstairs hallway, and despite my every effort to the contrary, my gaze strays upward.

I'm supposed to be smarter than that, too. Smart enough not to want my little brother's girlfriend.

Would it have killed him to pick anyone other than Daughtry Sutcliffe? Not that she notices me. Or that I have the courage to ask her out.

I'd tutored her a few times in the fall, during the grape harvest. We held a traditional crush as a promotional event, and she'd been the first to dive into the vat. She was new in town, but fearless. Captivating. The dark purple juice had splattered her dark blonde hair and run down her pale arms in rivulets. I still remembered the shirt she had worn that day, a nearly threadbare Fleetwood Mac concert tee. I was mesmerized by her. For weeks she was all I thought about after I'd gone back to school. I almost hadn't turned in my grad school applications on time, because I'd been so wrapped up in her.

When she asked me to tutor her in chemistry, I thought that was my shot. The few rare hours with her had been perfect. Symphonic. The two of us huddled over notebooks and texts, the sounds of our laughter drowning out the scratching of our pencils. I wanted to ask her out. There was this moment...I thought she had given me an in.

But she hadn't.

Turned out it was all an excuse for her to meet my younger brother. Story of my life.

My cock stirs, dazed and confused after the weeklong slog of studying for midterms here at my parents' house. The weeklong slog of avoiding my brother and Daughtry.

I grit my back teeth.

This is wrong. She's eighteen, a senior in high school, and I'm four years older than her. She is my brother's girlfriend.

My. Fucking. Brother's. Girlfriend.

Abandoning my banana ester compound, I stand from the kitchen table and beeline for the fridge. I need to eat something to settle my stomach. I yank on the fridge door, bathing in its warm glow and its soft hum. Nothing looks appealing. There's a bottle of blueberry hard cider beside the orange juice, but if I drink that, I'll never sleep properly.

Only two more days. Two more days of this torture and then I will head back to college. I'll pass my classes, attend parties where I know less than ten people, and graduate. I will put miles and miles and miles between me and my brother and his luscious girlfriend.

I never would have come home if I'd known my parents would be out of town, leaving me and my brother alone with Daughtry. And I would have left early, really I would have, except my dorm is full of people who will make it even more impossible to study.

I'm fucked, in all except the literal way.

"Oops!" A female voice says behind me, followed by a tinkling laugh.

I slam the fridge door closed, revealing Daughtry.

My mouth waters, and it has nothing to do with anything I've seen in the fridge. Daughtry's blond hair is up in a high, messy ponytail, her pale cheeks are flushed, and her golden hazel eyes flash with amusement. She holds a fraying black leather handbag covered in metal studs in one hand and a pair of worn Converse sneakers in the other. They have little hand-made stars on them in glittery puffy paint. "Hi, Declan. Sorry, I didn't know you were still awake."

"Mmhm," I say, but it sounds more like "Mvensnup." Wonderful. Way to sell college, Smart Guy. I used to be able to speak actual words. "Hi, Daughtry." I stick my hands in my back pockets before remembering that, unfortunately, I'm wearing sweatpants and there are no back pockets. Having smacked my own ass unintentionally, I ignore it like a pro and lean against the fridge. "I'm just studying."

"Midterms. Right." She pulls her bottom lip between her teeth as she glances over at my mountain of study materials, including empty bags of chips and cookies and soda cans. I have an intense urge to one-arm sweep everything into a trash bag and then throw myself in, too. What was I thinking, leaving such a mess when I knew she was upstairs? "College. So close and yet so far away."

She's talking to me. Daughtry Sutcliffe, who has haunted my dreams more than once, is having an actual conversation with me. I have to think of something to say. Anything. Anything besides the truth, because it would be one thousand percent inappropriate to tell my brother's girlfriend that I think I'm in love with her.

"Are you thinking about college?" *Yes!* Finally, for the first time in my life, I say something that fits the situation.

"Yes." Her eyes twinkle and she moves across the kitchen like she owns it. I would happily have given it to her, if it were mine to give. She has gorgeous feet, petite and capable. They're how I picture a dancer's feet. Except one time sophomore year I had dated a dancer, and she did *not* have cute feet.

That is completely beside the point.

"I'm NYC bound, baby!" She punches the air like a prize fighter and it is the cutest thing I've ever seen.

"That's awesome." She will be thousands of miles away from my brother, which seems like a mark in the plus column. "Congratulations."

"Thanks, Declan." She paws through the bags of snacks on the table, but she isn't going to find anything. I'm a scarfer when I study. No junk food is safe. "I'm pretty excited. I've been researching affordable voice coaches and everything. My mom doesn't want me to major in music, but I have a scholarship, so she doesn't get a say. Like I don't get a say in her life." Leaving the table, she moves across to the cupboards. She's like a restless little hamster. No, something cuter than a hamster. A quokka?

I'm hopeless.

"Are you hungry?" I ask. Damn Ciaran. Had he even offered her water after hooking up with her? Of course he wouldn't have thought of that. I mentally schedule a Very Serious Chat with my brother for tomorrow on the proper care of women. I move to the fridge and take out a can of soda and a bottle of water. "Want a drink? I can make pancakes."

"Ooh." Daughtry plucks the soda can from my hand and pops it with one nail covered in chipped teal polish. "You're only confirming that you're the sensitive brother."

That stings. Sensitive brothers don't get the girl. "Pancakes sound good. I always study better with a full stomach." I busy myself with getting the pancake mix and filling a measuring cup with water from the tap. I'm not avoiding looking at her. No. Of course not.

I turn to put the measuring cup in the sink and Daughtry sits in one of the bar stools at the kitchen island, her legs in her skintight jeans swinging in the air. Her elbows rest on the island, cradling her heart-shaped face in her hands.

She has a line of piercings in her left ear, little hearts and moons and gems running along the curve. I memorize each one. They almost look like a chemical compound winding along her cartilage.

I am most definitely staring. I pay attention to the stove instead and turn on the electric cooktop, sliding my mom's ancient cast iron pan into place on the burner.

"No one's ever made me pancakes before," Daughtry says

quietly, her tone holding a hint of amusement. Daughtry always looks like that, like she's about to burst into laughter, or a joyful Broadway number, complete with sparkly costume. "I guess, technically, restaurants make pancakes for you. No one's ever made them in their house for me."

The skin along my hands heats, which has nothing to do with the stove or the butter melting into the pan. I don't know much about Daughtry's mom, but I've inferred a lot. She spends a lot of time at the Broken Lighthouse, and she is neither bartender nor waitress there.

"I don't think Ciaran knows how to turn on the stove, but I can teach him. He should make you breakfast." Though that brings up all the reasons why my little brother would be making her breakfast, which only makes me see her in the vat, her thin T-shirt soaked with grape juice and clinging to her curves. I grip the spatula so tightly that the metal wand falls out of the plastic handle. I rush to reassemble it.

"Pfft." Daughtry picks up the napkins and starts folding them into different shapes, origami boats and fans. "He brought me pretzels once. Is it weird? Talking about your brother's sex life?"

Yes. "No. Of course not." I ladle some of the pancake batter into the cast iron, but instead of the sun I wanted to make, it spreads into an amoeba. Amoebas are easier to contemplate than what Daughtry and my brother do up in his room while our parents are out of town.

"What about you?" she asks.

I spoon another scoop of batter into the foaming butter. This one spreads into a shape like a used condom. Great. That sends all the right messages. "What about me?" I use the edge of the spatula to nudge it out of the used condom shape and into more of a trapezoidal bubble.

"I bet you pull all kinds of women at college."

All the hairs on the back of my neck stand erect. My hand

stumbles and I slice the trapezoidal bubble into two irregular triangles. Her gaze is a laser. Why would she ask me that? I shouldn't think about it. "Despite what pop culture wants you to believe, the nerdy guy doesn't get the girl." Mostly because nerdy guys have to study in order to keep their scholarships and get into graduate programs, because a plain old Bachelor of Science degree is worth about as much as a steaming pile of B.S.

"I can't believe that. You're smart, hot, and you know how to make pancakes. I'll bet you have all the ladies lined up outside your dorm room."

I sneak a look at her when I reach up into the cupboard to get a plate. Her hazel gaze is on me, watching my every move. It's enough to clear all the organic chemistry from my brain.

I'm not a monk, of course not. But do I have the kind of pull my younger brother has? Hell no. Certainly not anyone of Daughtry's caliber.

I focus on transferring the cooked pancakes to a plate, and remember all the reasons why this isn't actually happening. She isn't flirting with me. She is just hungry. She is too young. She is out of my league.

She is my brother's girlfriend.

I hand the plate to her across the island and then take the bottle of syrup out of the fridge. "Yum," she says, licking her lips. With the prongs of her fork, she traces the outline of the amoeba-like one. "This one looks like an amoeba. Or maybe a raincloud."

My cock swells, and I hide my growing erection with the stove. Pancakes. I can make fucking pancakes and not get hard thinking about her. It's wrong. Very wrong, and I am a very, very bad man for even remotely contemplating it.

Very bad.

Pancake batter splashes into the sizzling hot pan in a

sequence of irregular blobs, not dissimilar to my banana ester model.

"These pancakes are delicious," Daughtry says. I hear her eating behind me. She has an incredible mouth, especially when she sings. Lips that curve around a microphone like she—

No. Pancakes. I am focusing on pancakes.

"I'll drive you home. It's too late to ride your bike." I lean against the counter, mostly so I don't fall into the hot butter and burn myself. "Unless Ciaran is going to drive you."

She snorts and leaps off her stool, holding her plate and soda can. "If my mom could save more than ten dollars at a time, I'd buy a car and save everyone the trouble." She puts her dishes in the sink and the can in the recycling. She turns to me, leaning her elbows back on the counter. The posture pushes her excellent breasts into a more prominent position, and I studiously keep my gaze on the pancakes.

Two of which sit in little circles right next to each other, looking remarkably like breasts.

I tug at the collar of my St. Olaf High Mathletes tee. "It's no trouble to drive you." My pancakes are burning. I flip them and settle them onto a plate. "I'd rather do that than worry about you."

I turn to get a fork from the drawer beside her, and this is a colossal mistake. Her gaze is on me, her eyes soft, her lips pulling into a gentle smile. The utensil drawer is a minefield. I don't need a fork. I can eat pancakes with my hands.

Before I can save myself, Daughtry circles one of her petite hands around my wrist. The bracelet of her touch burns and nearly makes me collapse like a skeleton-less sack. My gaze, tortured traitor that it is, trails from her hand up to her face and arrests there. She is the most beautiful woman I've ever seen.

"You're a really nice guy, aren't you, Declan?" Her voice is a sultry promise.

My breath stutters in my chest. "That sounds like a kiss of death."

She leans a centimeter closer to me. She smells like maple syrup and my brother's soap and it's all very confusing. My cock doesn't know how to make heads or tails of it, but it follows thousands of years of genetic code and rises to the occasion. "You could look at it as a kiss of hope. Some girls do want nice guys, Declan." I love the way she says my name, like it's music.

Still. I know the truth. She is Ciaran's girlfriend.

I step away from her and set the pancakes on the island by the stove. Distance would be helpful in this situation. "What does Ciaran think about you moving to New York?"

Daughtry scoffs. "You and I both know he won't give a shit. He's great, really. But it won't last, and I'm cool with that."

My only two girlfriends so far have both been of the long-term monogamous variety. I'm not built for the casual hook up. But how could Ciaran ever let Daughtry get away? If she were mine...but she isn't.

"You are?" I ask. "Cool with that?"

She shrugs. "If I'm going to be a songwriter, I need a lot of different experiences to pull from. I need to write about life, and there's no way to do that unless I live it. These feet are not designed to stay put. And besides, no one wants songs about the person they settled for in high school." Her gaze flicks up and down my body, and not for the first time, I wish I were wearing something other than study sweats. "Don't you think?"

The whole kitchen feels charged, filled with crackling energy, protons and electrons flittering around at warp speeds. The air is sweet with the scent of pancakes and rich fried butter and sugary maple syrup. Through it all, there is Daughtry, pulling me to her like she always does.

What if this once I took a chance? Not to kiss her or have sex or anything, but to share time with her? Get to know her? The instant slips through my fingers like water through a sieve.

But I want it to last. I step toward her. "Daughtry—"

"Hey, are those pancakes?" My asshole brother stomps into the room, sweeps up the plate of pancakes I had made, then bends and kisses Daughtry full on the lips. He is shirtless and wearing a pair of boxer shorts that my mom should have made him throw away, since they are at least two sizes too small. I imagine he didn't because he likes how tight they are. "Ooh, these ones look like boobs. Don't they, babe?" He tilts his plate for Daughtry to look. She glances down briefly then back up toward me.

"Yeah. Sure, Ciaran," she says.

Kicking myself, I turn off the stove and take a bottle of water back to my study table. That's all over. I had one chance to tell her how I felt, and I blew it.

"I'll drive you home in two minutes, babe," Ciaran says. I hear him kiss Daughtry again, sloppy and loud. Like a douche.

I bend my head back to my banana ester model.

I blew my one chance and I will never get another one.

CHAPTER 2

 aughtry—Now

I NEVER THOUGHT I'd be here again.

Of all the places my mom and I had lived growing up, I always liked St. Olaf the most. Which is why I never intended to return. Life is in the front windshield, not the rear view mirror.

"Daughtry, we have to prepare your statements for the interview." My agent, Louise Fields, scrolls down her tablet screen. "It's the local paper, but still. They want to talk about when you lived here, what it's like to be back, blah blah. What do you want to say about Wisconsin and your time here?"

Outside the car, familiar fields and trees fly by. A warm sense of nostalgia curls in my stomach. "It's so green." Los Angeles is the place I've lived the longest over the last decade, but it's brown grass and sprawling buildings for eight months out of the year. Here it's lush and rich, the air thicker. I like it. It feels...real.

Louise follows my gaze briefly, then glances back down at her tablet. Her hands, dark brown with golden undertones, speed over the screen. "My allergies are already acting up. You cannot just comment on the colors unless you want to be poetic or for them to think you're high. Are you high?"

"No, of course not." That's one of Louise's conditions. No drugs. I have zero issues following that stipulation. Drugs and alcohol are not my coping mechanisms. Anonymous sex is another story, but this is small town Wisconsin. That's not going to happen and I won't need it out here.

All my stressors are elsewhere, for the first time in a long time.

"Good." She nods once, her tight, dark brown spirals held back on one side with a clip. "So what else?"

"I don't know." I remember that road. That leads to the trailer park where my mom and I lived for my senior year of high school. Not that either of us spent much time there. "A lot of my most popular songs were written from experiences here. I could talk about that."

"Perfect." Louise arches one artfully-plucked brow, tapping notes onto her screen with admirable efficiency. "And the guy? There was a guy, right?"

My stomach churns as I stare out the window. The road leading to the Fosters' vineyard is up on the right.

I turn my head to face the front windshield. "There's always a guy, isn't there? One who got away."

"WHAT DO YOU MEAN, the apartment is booked?" Louise stares down the woman with dark brown eyes and gray-streaked hair who looked half-Korean.

Maddy Olmstead shrugs, her light blue cardigan slipping

down her shoulders. "I'm so sorry." She slides her cellphone into the back pocket of her wide-leg jeans. She is petite and dressed comfortably, and looks exactly the same as when I'd lived here in high school. Not that I spent a ton of time at the town library, where Maddy works. "It's the Rock and Wine Festival, and there must have been a mixup with the online reservation system. You just can't trust technology now, believe you me. It's like quality control is an afterthought now."

I stand to the side, staring at the cozy cottage with vines covering the pale yellow walls. There is a trellis of climbing roses to one side of the house, and a small vegetable garden with beans and tomatoes growing up their frames. Seasons in Los Angeles become so jumbled together. I've forgotten what a real August looks like.

Sultry, hazy, long days filled with the scents of stolen summer kisses.

That's one of the many reasons I'm excited for this tour. I need to get out of the city, away from my bad habits. My feet have been itching to be anywhere else, and the constant motion of the road is what I've been craving. I needed to base myself in LA for my music career, but now that it's finally rocketing, I need to experience...*more.*

Louise rubs the space between her eyes, her brow wrinkled in a way she would never normally allow. "Do you have any idea if there are openings anywhere else in town?"

Maddy shakes her head. "I'm not sure. Most places around town have been booked for months. One of the vineyards might have a spot, if you call around. Some of them are renting places now. You could try Foster Family Vineyards."

My abdomen clenches.

"Thank you." Louise sighs loudly and turns to me. "I'm so sorry, Daughtry. Your first tour opening for the Vendetta and your accommodation is screwed."

"It's fine." It really is. I trust Louise. After having heard horror stories of other managers, Louise is a unicorn in the music industry. Supportive, hardworking, and she doesn't run me into the ground.

Louise is already searching on her phone. "Let me see if I can find the number for that vineyard."

"No!" I've spoken too sharply. Both Maddy and Louise stare at me with widened eyes.

I wave my hand in the air and inhale the scent of St. Olaf. I'd forgotten that, too. How it smells in the summer like ripe fruit and lazy humid days by the lakeside. "Really, don't worry, Louise. Something will turn up. Aren't we going to be late getting to the festival grounds?"

"You're right." Louise's gaze fixes on the paddock in the distance, where a palomino and a bay thoroughbred graze. Is Louise a horse person? I thought she grew up in Pennsylvania, not that her birthplace makes her less likely to be a horse person. Asking would involve crossing my own personal boundaries.

She rolls her shoulders back and turns to me, smiling. "Everything is going to go great this weekend. We'll find you somewhere to stay. You'll wow everyone tomorrow night when you open for the Vendetta, you'll sell every single piece of merch we brought, and the world will be your oyster."

"Thank you for the pep talk." My phone buzzes in my pocket but I ignore it.

Louise, however, does not. With her gaze narrowed, she points a dagger-like fingernail at my cell phone. "Is your mom calling again?"

Busted. "I'm sticking to what we agreed. Really. I don't send her any more. I don't answer more than once a day."

Maddy scoffs loudly, then coughs to cover it up. Apparently people here in town remember my mother.

Oh goody.

Louise sighs. "Don't let toxicity into your life, Daughtry. There are enough people in this industry—hell, in this world —who will try to bring you down. Find the ones who lift you up."

"Amen," Maddy Olmstead agrees.

It sounds easy, and I grin with them in solidarity. But inside, my stomach is like an empty pit.

I don't have people to fill the voids in my life. I have temporary hook ups to scratch the itch, and people I work with, acquaintances I call friends. But the last people who had truly known me live here, in St. Olaf, Wisconsin.

And I am in no way prepared to see them again.

CHAPTER 3

 eclan—Now

"ALEX!" I slather peanut butter on one slice of wheat bread and my mom's homemade raspberry jam on another. "We have to go!"

"School doesn't start for two more weeks, Dad!" he calls down the stairs.

He's going to wake up my mom. That's exactly what she needs while she tries to convert the guest cottage into a vacation rental property.

"I know that." I wrap the sandwich with reusable beeswax-lined cloth and place the whole thing into a lunch box. "But we have to get to the fairgrounds to set up the tasting tent. I promised your grandparents. May I remind you that you love them more than me." I raise my tone on the last sentence, hoping it carries to my nine-year-old son's increasingly selective hearing.

"He also loves me more than you." Ciaran waltzes into the

kitchen wearing nothing but boxer shorts. "Did you make breakfast?" He reaches for the blueberry bran muffins I made, but I snatch the plate away.

"These are for my kid. Get your own breakfast."

"You are way too uptight," Ciaran says. He yanks open the freezer and pulls out a container of frozen fruits and veggies. He carries this to the blender and dumps the contents in. "You need to get laid, man. Josie left two years ago."

I fill up two water bottles with ice, rolling my eyes. Getting laid is not a possibility. We live in a town where there are no unmarried women my age, at least none I haven't known since we were in diapers together. "Who am I going to have sex with, Ciaran? Maddy Olmstead?"

"She may be in her sixties, but she looks like she'd be a beast." Ciaran pours almond milk into the blender, covers it, and hits the smoothie button. "I'm pretty sure she and Opal are together, though."

"I'm a single dad. What am I supposed to do?" I finish packing the lunches and water bottles into my backpack.

"Do what other single parents do. Let me and the 'rents watch the squirt, who honestly is old enough to watch himself, and go to Chicago for the weekend to dust off your Tinder."

"Do you learn to speak in code at search and rescue?" I stick a mug under the drip from the coffee machine. "And nine is not old enough to watch himself."

Ciaran elbows me out of the way to grab the sugar. "You're not that old, dude. You know what fucking Tinder is."

"Language, boys." Our mom, Zoe Foster, walks in carrying a laundry basket filled with clean sheets. "You're both over thirty. Can you not act like you're three? Ciaran, how's the cottage? Is it ready for guests yet?"

"Yes, Mom. It's filled with all the bougie shit you wanted." Ciaran pours his purple-colored smoothie into a glass.

Mom's eyes narrow with exasperation. "It's not bougie. It's tasteful. That Remodel Your Home and Life seminar your dad and I went to, down at the VFW, recommended the blackout curtains and said everyone is doing heated bathroom floors and towel racks. Especially here in Wisconsin. I think I want them for this house, too, if the rental property starts paying out." She drops the laundry basket by the sliding glass doors that open onto the backyard. "Declan, do you have everything packed for the festival tasting booth?"

"Got it all in the truck out back."

She pats me on the cheek as she walks by me. "That's my responsible boy. Where's Alex?"

"Taking his time!" I call upstairs. Breakfast. The kid needs breakfast. I have the muffins for him, but I take the cereal from the cupboard and two bowls from the drawer beside the sink. Just in case he decides he doesn't like blueberries today.

Footsteps pound down the stairs, far heavier than any sixty pound child should sound. "Dad!" Alex barrels into the room, grabbing the cereal box from me as he rushes past. "Tell me what I can do to earn more screen time during the week. I *need* to be able to Minecraft. I can't just play on the weekends. What can I do?"

I hand him the almond milk. "Emancipation."

Alex screws up his face, looking so much like Ciaran when he was nine and being a tool. He inherited his mother's blond hair, and somehow his uncle's stubborn streak. "I don't know what that is, Dad."

"And that is exactly why you can't have more screen time. You need to read actual books."

Ciaran snickers into the dregs of his smoothie. "You sound like such a teacher, Dec."

"I am a teacher. Even when I'm helping out with the family business during the summer."

Mom walks back through the kitchen with another laundry basket, this one filled with succulents in colorful pots. "We really appreciate it, hon."

"I'd help, too, but, you know, fire department. No rest for us wicked hot guys." Ciaran swipes the bowl of cereal I had poured for myself and takes a seat beside Alex. "Hey, squirt nut, are you excited for the festival?" He spoons a large scoop of my cereal into his mouth.

I stare at the plate of healthy, freshly baked blueberry bran muffins, sitting forlorn on the kitchen island. Nobody wants my muffins. Story of my life.

I pull out another bowl and tilt the box into it, but only a few flakes drift into my bowl. Wonderful. Whoop dee fricking doo. I'm stuck with the blueberry bran muffins. That is an unexpected thing about being a dad. I think way too much about fiber.

"I'm pretty excited." Alex pauses in eating his cereal and examines his nails, which he has painted in alternating colors of teal, black, and lavender. "I really want to see the Vendetta."

"Their music is awesome." Ciaran polishes off the cereal and leans backward in the chair. "And their lead singer? Ellery? Totally hot. But you know who the real story is at this Rock and Wine Fest?"

"No." Alex brings his empty bowl to the sink without me prompting, which almost makes me want to reward him with screen time.

Ciaran smirks, which is not a reach for his face, as it is the expression he's most likely to settle into. "Daughtry Sutcliffe."

The jar of peanut butter I'm holding slides from my

hands and bounces once on the floor. Thanks to the industrial grade plastic, nothing is broken.

"I like her songs. I've heard 'Grape Crush' before. It has a really good beat." Alex bobs his head. Today he is wearing one of his favorite shirts, forest green with a large black video game controller printed on the front.

"I'm not going to brag." Ciaran stretches his arms up and over his head. "But a lot of those songs she wrote? They're about me. We dated during senior year of high school."

The bread I'm trying to spread with raspberry jam keeps tearing. Damn knife. I switch it out for a spatula, but I dig a crater in the center of the bread slice. "She dated a lot of people, Ciaran. You can't be that memorable."

Ciaran rolls his eyes. "Please. *'He's the one I never told, and the one who warms me when it's cold?'* That's totally me. She never told me she loved me before she left, so she wrote it all in song."

It's difficult to see my breakfast through the haze encroaching on my vision. One would think that twelve years would be enough time to forget that night when I made Daughtry pancakes.

One would be terribly, horribly, irrevocably wrong.

"Do you know her, Dad?" Alex looks at me as though he finally finds me interesting, and it scars and buoys me simultaneously.

Unfortunately for my ego, I have vowed never to lie to my son. "A little. I tutored her once or twice."

Ciaran walks over to the coffee pot and selects a mug from the wooden tree beside it. "I always thought your dad had a little thing for her. She was H-O-T hot back then. And she chose the superior brother. I love your dad, but he's never had much game."

My fists clench, overwhelmed with the urge to hit him. "Stop, Ciaran."

Ciaran fills his mug then picks up the creamer and adds a generous amount. "Stop what? The kid's gotta learn who to go to when he wants to learn how to pull."

I cross my arms over my chest. They twitch against my breastbone. "He's nine."

"He'll be on Twitch with some hot young thang chatting him up in no time."

"You are a white man from Wisconsin. There is no universe in which you should say 'hot young thang.' And stop talking about my kid."

"Don't talk about me like I'm not here, Dad," Alex says. His brow furrows, giving me yet another hopeless glimpse into his teenage future. Great. I'm failing him. I'm failing at this. I've tried so hard for so long and it's all going to crash and burn.

Mom walks back through the kitchen, this time holding her gardening shoes in one hand and a spray bottle of cleanser in the other. "None of you should speak like this to each other. We're family. I have to go out to clean the guest cottage, so behave." With that, she steps into the backyard and shuts the door.

The three of us resume our battle positions.

Ciaran sips his coffee, almost casually. "You know, Alex, your dad is a great guy. Super smart. Very nice. But how he ever managed to bag a hottie like your mom is anyone's guess."

I smack him upside his head. "Don't talk about his mom like that, Ciaran."

"Don't hit me, dude." Ciaran crosses his arms over his chest and pops his pecs. How exactly am I related to this douchebag? "I can totally take you."

I stand stock still, leaning against the kitchen island. "I'm not fighting you in front of my kid."

"Dad, if I take your side, can I have screen time?" Alex

folds his hands together in prayer position and pinches his face into a pleading puppy expression. "Please please?"

Fuck it. I'm done. "Fine. Get in the car and you can play Minecraft while I set up the tasting tent. As long as you promise not to tell Grams anything that just happened."

CHAPTER 4

 aughtry

WITH MY HEADPHONES on and plugged into my guitar, I run through the riffs in "Grape Crush." I don't need Louise reminding me that this is my big break. Touring with the Vendetta is a dream, and it's taken twelve years of hustle, blood, and sweat to get here.

I'm not going to mess it up by slipping on my chord progressions.

Dante Baker, the bassist for the Vendetta, stops in front of me and waves his hand in front of my face. He's dressed as he always is, in a button down shirt and trim jeans.

"Hey." I slip my headphones down around my neck. "How's it going, Dante?"

"Not too bad." He pushes his shaggy dark hair out of his eyes. "Have you seen Ellery?"

"No, sorry." With the hand not holding my guitar, I

gesture around the lake. "This resort is gorgeous, isn't it? Are you staying here?"

He shakes his head. "Ellery has some friends with a vacation house nearby, so Louise didn't book our accommodations. What about you?"

"Not sure. We went to the rental apartment, but the owner told us there was a glitch in the system so it was double booked. Louise is looking into it now. All the hotels in the area are booked for the festival." So what if Foster Family Vineyards may have an opening? I'm not running headfirst into that minefield.

"Makes sense." Dante rocks back on his feet, looking uncomfortable at talking to anyone beyond his bandmates for more than five minutes. "I'm going to find Ellery. Do you want to come?"

"Sure." I hop off the packing crate I've been perching on and replace my guitar in its case. "It's been ages since I lived here, but I remember the food being incredible."

We walk from the concert stage that has been set up by the conference center and down among the maze of tent-lined lanes. I love festivals. They smell like deep fried heaven and warm summer rain. This one has the added benefit of excellent music piped through the speakers.

I grab Dante's arm. "Hold on. I know this song."

It's the Vendetta's first and most famous single, "Centrifuge."

"How cool!" The lyrics wash over me. The first time I ever heard the song was on *America Sings!* and I was completely hooked. "I can't wait until that's me."

"It will be, one day. Honestly, it's weird, hearing our songs on the radio," Dante says. One of the nicest things about him is that he isn't that tall, only a few inches more than me, so I never feel dwarfed.

"I spent so long trying to get to this stage and now it all just feels like quicksand," I say.

"You'll settle into it. We all do." We pass by a tent with local metalwork jewelry. Dante pauses, sifting through the earrings. He holds up a pair made of bronze and silver hammered ovals. "Do you think Ellery will like these?"

"Yes." I run my fingers over the studs in my left ear. I got the piercings senior year of high school, and I rarely take them out. For a while, it was from lack of money. If I had spare cash, it usually went to food or transportation back then. Then I didn't change them because I kind of liked remembering how Zoey Foster had noticed them immediately. The day I got them, she'd stepped back to examine them properly, her face lit up with appreciation. It had made me feel so seen.

I still don't think my actual mother knew or noticed. I've definitely never told her about my other piercings. "You and Ellery are definite couple goals. I don't think a guy has ever picked out jewelry for me that I actually liked." Not that I give them a chance. Better not to be disappointed.

Dante hands the earrings to the seller and taps his card on the credit card reader. "I used to think no one would ever love me for who I am. But Ellery gets me. In that deep, soul-satisfying way."

It's either fear or indigestion that makes my fingers feel numb. It isn't the memory of how, when Zoey asked for her son Declan's opinion on my new earrings, his gaze darkened and he'd said, *She already looked like a superstar.*

I pick up a pendant of a dragon and then put it right back on its tree-shaped jewelry stand. "I mean, deep and soul-satisfying is one way to live. Or you can try to cram as many experiences as possible into life. Who's to say which is better?"

"That's true." He takes the little green jewelry bag from

the seller and puts it in the pocket of his dark wash jeans. The color washes his pale skin out more, but he has a look that he likes. "There are a lot of different ways to live. You have to find your own joy."

"Exactly."

"Hey, there she is." His face explodes into a wide smile as Ellery comes into view, perusing a used book stall. "I'll see you later, Daughtry. You're going to be great." With very little fanfare, he walks toward Ellery and slips his arms around her waist. Ellery laughs and leans back against his chest.

Way too much intimacy.

The scent of fried food makes me feel woozy. I walk away from the obscenely happy couple. There are distractions aplenty here, and I need one desperately. There are so many memories here, more than other places I've lived, like New York or Nashville. Even Los Angeles. Though I've been in California for years now, the city is so huge and sprawling, that it never really feels like I'm in the same place.

Still. St. Olaf has its small town charm. And it goes all out for festivals.

I pass lemonade stands, cream puffs that are larger than my head, and a stall selling Renaissance Faire-style flower garlands. The air smells like grilled meats and onions and sugar wafts in the air like sweet-scented smoke.

Closer to the lake, there is a white fence surrounding a series of tents, with white wooden benches and long tables set up inside the perimeter. Over the little gate, manned by an ancient white man with a serious farmer's tan, is a sign in curlicue writing: Biergarten, over 21 only.

I'm not much of a drinker, but there is a sentimental pull to Wisconsin's local breweries and cideries. Vineyards, too.

It was twelve years. Who am I kidding? The Fosters probably left town ages ago.

Although, in a weird spell after I broke up with my last

boyfriend—we passed our three date termination mark—I looked up the Foster brothers on social media. Declan's profile was private, but his mom's is public. She had posted photos from a Mother's Day celebration, complete with a little nine-year-old mini Ciaran. The brothers had both aged well, Declan especially. I'm surprised Ciaran has a kid. I would have pegged Declan as the paternal one of the two. He was definitely the Relationship Material brother.

Has Declan ever married?

A little kernel of want curls deep in my core but I push it aside. That's ancient history and there's no good bringing any of it back.

"ID, please?" The bouncer, who could not weigh more than a hundred and twenty pounds soaking wet—and may have been that old—holds out a hand to me.

"Sure." My badge identifying me as a performer isn't going to cut it in this setting. I dig through my ancient leather messenger bag until I find my wallet. "Here you go." I hand him my driver's license.

He peruses it with the same care a person might give to reading the Declaration of Independence for the first time. It's oddly touching. "Hmph. All right, Ms. Sutcliffe. Drink responsibly, now."

"I will." What a wild place. I get carded everywhere in LA, too, but nobody seems to care there. It's more of a perfunctory glance. I read his name badge and flash him my stage smile. "Thanks, Frank."

He opens the gate for me and I walk into the Biergarten. I've been in a lot of these, too, throughout my childhood. If I have to pick a table, the one over by the craft beer tent would be my mom's. Not because of its impressive selection of IPAs. It looks like it has the softest grass underneath to curl up for an impromptu drunk nap.

Tucking my performer badge beneath the collar of my

navy blue ribbed tank top, I walk around reading the signs. Altenbosch Orchard Cider. Golden Rose Brewery. Sweet Valley Vines.

I don't realize I'm looking for it until it's right in front of me. Foster Family Vineyards.

Nobody is working the tent, thank heaven and hell and anyone else who's listening. A dark, lush green runner lined the tasting table, and there is a chalkboard on either end listing the wines available to taste. Heart Stomp Chardonnay. Frozen Out Ice Wine.

Yeesh. Someone was going through something when they named these wines.

A tow-headed kid wearing neon blue eyeshadow pops up from beneath the table. He eyes me warily, blue eyes calculating. "My dad names the wines."

Wow. This is such a mini Ciaran.

"Who broke your dad's heart?" I ask.

"My dad is unbreakable."

Respect. "Right on, kid. What's your name?"

"Alex." He stretches out his hand to me and I take it in mine. His palm is a little sticky but he gives my hand one good, firm shake. "What can I getcha?"

I lean on the table on my elbows. "Aren't you a little young to be serving wine?"

"Please." Alex rolls his eyes. "I live on a vineyard. I could tell you more than any sommelier in Napa."

Somehow, I believe him. He projects confidence. "Okay. Wow me."

Unimpressed. That describes Alex perfectly. He pulls a thin bottle of honey-colored liquid from underneath the table. "Try our ice wine. It's my favorite."

"Alex." A dark-haired man enters the back of the tent, carrying a clanking box full of wine bottles. "You know you're not supposed to be serving. I'm so sorry, I'll be right

—"

Whoa. It's like all the air in the tent condenses and expands at once. When he starts speaking, that deep, rich tone sizzles down my spine. How it is possible for that one glimpse of him to make me shiver, I have no idea.

But I'm not one to linger.

"Hey, Declan," I say. Do I pop my chest out a little bit? Maybe. I have a back ache.

His eyes widen and he drops the box of wine, a little too heavily on the ground. It seems okay. No telltale signs of leaking grape juice. Then again, what do I know? "Daughtry? Is that you?"

Has it really been twelve years? He looks just as good as the last time I saw him, at Ciaran and my high school graduation. He is tall and rangy. He has dark brown hair that is longer on top than the sides, and these cyan-colored eyes that flit from dark as a stormy lake to bright summer sky. He has mood eyes, Declan Foster does.

"Hey, stranger."My entire body is restless, like there are fire ants crawling along my skin. As much as my head screams *run*, my itchy feet are planted firmly on the ground.

Screw it. I ignore convention, leap over the tasting table, and wrap my arms around Declan.

Mistake. Declan smells like cherries and fresh linen and clean summer air. And the hug he gives me? It takes him a moment of hesitation, but when his arms enclose me, it feels a lot like security. Comfort.

I release a breath that feels about twelve years old.

This is very dangerous. The pull of him here is so strong, and holding him floods me with memories.

Mentally, I reinforce all my inner walls, but the mortar I typically use isn't sticking when Declan holds me like this. I need a new plan and quick.

But...*cherries.*

"Dad?" Alex says behind us. "Who is she?"

"Oh." Declan steps away from me, a flush running up his pale, untanned neck. He's let his five o'clock shadow grow so it covers his cheeks in a sexy unkempt way, like a *GQ* model.

Sexy? No. Not sexy. Devastating.

A warm puddle of want collects inside my belly. While I normally keep my emotions tightly behind lock and key à la Fort Knox, if I spend more time with Declan, I'll need to upgrade to Vegas casino-level security.

He puts at least two feet between us, an impressive thing given that the entire tent isn't that wide. "Alex, this is Daughtry. She dated your uncle Ciaran their senior year of high school."

A thousand things click into place. Of course Alex isn't Ciaran's. I knew Ciaran doesn't have a paternal bone in his body. Now that I look past the blond hair, I see Declan in Alex's eyes, in his posture.

"You're not telling the whole story." I turn to Alex, who seems moderately more interested in me now. "One night, even though your dad was studying for midterms, he made me the world's best pancakes."

"My dad does make really good pancakes. He says it's all in the mix." Alex glances between the two of us for a moment before he catches sight of my performer badge. Hugging Declan dislodged it from behind my tank top. "Shit, you're Daughtry Sutcliffe!"

"Alex, don't swear," Declan says, as if this is an automated response. It's fricking adorable.

"But Dad!" Alex has a little vocal fry that he uses to great effect. I respect him for it. "You told me you 'sort of knew her.' You didn't tell me you made her pancakes."

Declan turns to the box of wine and starts unpacking the bottles without reading the labels. He's so fucking cute when he's flustered. That hasn't changed at all. "They were just pancakes."

"World's best pancakes." I lean my butt against the tasting table, now fully enjoying myself. With Declan kneeling on the ground beside the box, I appreciate the tone of his muscles, visible underneath his polo shirt. He's always been built, but age has settled well on him. "And we were friends. Your dad tutored me so I didn't fail chemistry in high school."

"You were never going to fail," Declan grumbles. He unpacks the box completely, and this seems only to distress him. Not looking at me, he picks up a box of wine glasses and starts setting them on the table. "You're too smart for that. You just needed to catch up a bit. Your last school was on a different track from ours."

Alex and I each take some of the glasses and set them up in a triangle shape on the other end of the table. "My dad teaches chemistry now," he says to me. "At the high school."

"I'll bet he's voted best teacher every year." And sexiest, not that I want to contemplate a gaggle of teens drooling over him. He has this whole lanky nerdy vibe going on. It's working for him.

"Pretty much." Alex shrugs. "So do you know the Vendetta?"

"Of course," I say. "I'm opening for them. It's the only reason I'm here. They're the coolest people."

Declan pulls on a leaf of the cardboard box, tearing it off with a flourish. He drops it, like ripping apart the box had not been his intention. "It's good to see you, Daughtry, but we have work to do. I'm sure you're busy, too."

I blow out a large puff of air, displacing my bangs into a little cascade of hair. "I have nowhere to go. The apartment they rented for me fell through and every other place was booked. It's me in the rental car. No big. I've done it before.

Besides." I pull my hair onto my head in a loose messy bun. "I can't leave before you tell me if you like the pink, Declan. It's new."

He glances briefly at me, and there is something so dark and fierce in his eyes, it pierces me to the spot. Some things do not change over twelve years. I never could tease Declan Foster. And flirting with him is a dangerous pastime. It reminds me of an iceberg, the way you can only see a little bit above the surface, but what's underneath is massive and sharp and potentially deadly.

"I like the pink," Alex says. He rests his chin in the palm of his hand as he contemplates my hair. "It's really cool. Dad, can I add pink streaks?"

"I'd rather you dye your hair than have more screen time, so sure." Declan tosses the empty box into a pile under the tablecloth.

"Whatever." This does not seem to be what Alex is hoping for. "Daughtry, you should stay with us."

"What?" Declan whirls on his son. "Alex, don't do that."

"Why not?" He raises his innocent little nine-year-old arms. "Grams says the place is finished now." He turns back to me. "Grams and Grampa turned our guest cottage into a vacation rental. You know, life on a vineyard thing. She had wanted to list it for the festival, but a water pipe burst so we couldn't take reservations. Don't worry, it's all fixed now so you don't have to wade through water or anything."

Who is this kid and how is he the coolest person I'd ever met? "Thank you."

Declan runs a hand over his face. "Alex, she does not want to stay at the vineyard. She's young and free and will prob-ably be up at all hours having—" he pauses here, like he's debating which insult will hit harder—" wild parties. She doesn't want to be saddled with us."

This was true earlier this morning, but now? I mean, I was invited. I'd hate to disappoint a child.

"Actually." I step neatly beside him, projecting my most innocent self. It isn't going to work. There's nothing innocent about me or the thoughts about Declan running through my head. "I'd love to stay with you. First of all, way better than sleeping in a car. It was fine in my twenties, but I'm thirty now and, technically, gainfully employed. I'd prefer not to wake up with back pain. Second—" I rustle Alex's hair, glowing in the beam he shoots my way—"your kid is amazing. If he wants to run away from you and all your shaking-your-newspaper-at-those-darn-neighbor-kids ways, he is totally welcome to stay with me in LA."

"Yes!" Alex says, but the ess is cut short by his father's glare.

This is way too much fun. There I go again, getting too close to the iceberg. I can't help it, though. Teasing Declan leads me into dangerous waters, but I'm in the boat now and steering directly toward it.

Sadly, it's exactly what my mother would have done.

"Third. The Vendetta would love to meet Alex." Cheap shot, playing the kid, but I've done worse. "I'd love to stay in your guest cottage. Let's say I have very fond memories of the place." Is this technically true? Yes. But it isn't a violation of my personal philosophy, either. I need a place to stay, and this is an excellent opportunity. "And for your very judgmental information, I don't party like that. No one in the Vendetta does, so I don't either. I like early nights, hot tea, and cozy blankets."

Declan's steel gaze softens a hair, but it could still poison like mercury. Slow and insidious.

"Fine," he grumbles, picking up a clean glass and wiping it with a washcloth. "I'll text my mom you're coming. But you're gone in two days, right?"

Two days until the festival is over and I'll be off to Chicago, Nashville, wherever Louise and the Vendetta tell me. Two days until I never see Alex or Declan again.

Still, life is for living. "Exactly." I pick up the bottle of Heart Stomp Chardonnay and pour myself a generous glass. "Two days and you'll never hear from me again."

CHAPTER 5

eclan

THE ABSOLUTE BEST way to distract a nine-year-old from asking questions about his parent's past is to stuff him full of Wisconsin's finest cream puffs. I'm not proud of it or looking forward to the inevitable sugar crash in about an hour, but it gives me a moment of peace, and I'll take it.

Alex and his friend Mac take their cream puffs and dash off to eat them where no one will offer them napkins. Which will have to be quite a distance away. If we didn't live in a small town where everyone knows both kids like they know their own, I would have placed a tracker on Alex.

"Hello, Declan." Marie Marshall, the head nurse at the local clinic, stands before me, wearing denim overalls and a brightly colored zigzag-patterned short sleeve shirt. She must have been out at the lake a lot that summer. Her normally white skin is tanned bronze.

"Hi, Marie. What can I getcha?" I set a clean glass before her.

"Whatever you're having." Her dark brown eyes twinkle. She doesn't mean anything by it. Marie still pines after her wife, who died twelve years ago.

"Sweet? Light? Blush?"

"I'll bet you make all the young ladies blush," Marie says kindly.

Not all. "Here, try the Swooning Dove Rosé. It's been popular, with the weather and all." I pour her a generous glass. This is the wine I thought Daughtry would like, not the Chardonnay. That's too heavy, too buttery. The rosé tastes of watermelon and strawberries. If my parents ever listened to me, they'd let me take the Chard grapes and age them in steel instead of oak. Or maybe amphora. An unoaked Chardonnay, styled like a Chablis, would suit Daughtry. A little classic, a little naughty.

No, not naughty. I'm not thinking anything naughty about Daughtry.

Marie swirls the pink liquid in her glass and raises it to her nose, inhaling deeply. "Oh, heck yes. This smells perfect." She takes a small sip, holding it on her tongue. "Delicious. Your family's outdone themselves."

I wave a hand. "It's not a competition." It is, mostly among the local vintners, and not for any sort of prestige beyond lording it over one another at hot ham and rolls on Sundays. "I'm glad you like it."

"Did you hear Daughtry Sutcliffe is back in town? Poor Maddy. She feels so badly about the mixup with the reservations."

Memories of Daughtry hugging me are not things I should contemplate while trying to upsell my family's wine. "Yeah, she stopped by earlier. She tried the Chardonnay."

"Her loss. Maybe next time you can convince her on the

rosé." Marie catches my gaze as she takes another healthy sip. "Will there be a next time, do you think? I always liked Daughtry. Shame she was here for only a year."

Small town gossip is one of the many things Josie hated about living here. Not the final straw, no. But a conversation like this would have made her snap pencils into tiny toothpicks. "Actually, Daughtry is going to be staying in my parents' guest cottage. Everywhere else is full, and we fixed that water leak." I wish someone else would stop by the tent to distract me, but it's barely noon and the real drinkers have not yet descended on the festival. Though I see Rove approaching. "So...She's staying with us."

Marie's eyes sparkle even more as she finishes off her rosé. "If that isn't making hay while the sun shines, I don't know what is, believe you me. I'll take a bottle of that rosé. Frannie and Laura will love it the next time we make paella."

I ring her up and place the bottle in a paper carrier bag for her. "Have a great day, Marie." I wave as she leaves.

Great. The news that Daughtry is staying Chez Foster will be all over town in three-point-two seconds.

I'M WRONG. It's one-point-two.

Ciaran rushes toward the tent. "Daughtry's staying in our guest cabin?"

I finish pouring a glass of Dumpster Fire Red Blend for Rove, the town's sanitation expert, before turning my attention to my brother. "Jeez, Ciaran. Did you burn your shirt along with the hamburgers?"

Ciaran glances down at his outfit, which consists of low slung jeans held up by red suspenders and nothing underneath. The man needs to hydrate more.

Unperturbed, Ciaran shrugs. "I didn't burn any burgers.

This time. And the fire department gets better tips if I serve shirtless."

"That's objectifying and concerns me for the state of our society." I ring up two bottles of rosé for Shirley Mott, our local high school principal.

Ciaran sidles up to the bar, reaches over the table, and pulls a can of blueberry hard cider out of the cooler. "You're missing the point. You saw Daughtry before I did and you got her to stay at our place?"

"Technically, it's not *your* place. How's that blend, Rove?" I ask. The ginger-haired man tilts his palm back and forth in the gesture version of *meh*. "Try the Cranbernet next. It's more your speed." My brother's energy sucks up all my attention, the asshole. "You have your own place. You're just at the vineyard all the time because you forget to buy groceries. And you enjoy making my life hell."

"My brother made my life hell." Rove drains the glass of not-bad red blend down his gullet. "That's why I ran him out of town."

That's a story I have no desire to hear. "Ciaran, I'm working. Don't you also have to work? People will be wanting their shirtless bratwurst." I hope the beer-steamed onions splash and burn his naked nipples.

Ciaran opens the can of cider and sips it. "Come on. You of all people know how hot and heavy Daughtry and I were. I always thought, if we didn't go off to separate colleges, we could really have made it work. You know?"

No. I don't know and I have no desire to know. The little I do know makes me want to burn my eyeballs with sulfuric acid.

This entire conversation makes my head buzz uncomfortably, like I'm stuck in a broken MRI machine.

"I'm working. Can we talk about this later?"

"Okay." Ciaran, in a first-of-its-kind gesture, places a

hand on my shoulder. "Thank you, bro. You're doing me a huge solid. I never knew you were this awesome of a wingman."

I wait until he and Rove are gone, then I take the bottle of red blend and empty it down my throat. Glasses are for winners, not unwilling wingmen.

CHAPTER 6

aughtry

"This place is amazing." Louise walks around the Fosters' guest cottage, admiring the furnishings. She has on a green, white, and black geometric print wrap dress and her black stilettos clack on the hardwood floors. "Daughtry, whatever guardian angel you have, can you share?"

"I'm so pleased you like it." Zoey Foster wrings a dish towel printed with rainbow-colored badgers between her freckled palms. She hasn't changed a bit. I circle the apartment, pretending to inspect it, but really I look at her.

If I could have chosen my ideal mom, it would have been Zoey Foster. Her ashy brown hair is a riot of curls around her head, and she still dresses like she's on her way to a yoga retreat. I find it all shockingly touching, so I keep my distance from her and Louise.

I trail a hand along the kitchen counter. Spotless. Who cleaned it? Declan? Zoey? It sure as hell wasn't Ciaran.

"We've done a lot of work to get it ready," Zoey says. "Daughtry, I'm honored you are our first guest."

"The honor is all mine, Zoey." Is it super awkward talking to my ex-boyfriend's mom? Less so than I'd expected. So far, it's also less of a minefield than talking with his gorgeous brother. "You've outdone yourself. You should be charging three times what you are."

The cottage is perfect. Everything is in shades of cream and pale green, but it's not a sickly, avocado color. More of a ripe Bartlett pear. There are two bedrooms, along with a kitchen and living area, in an open concept floor plan. On the hardwood, there are thick, faux fur rugs that make me want to lounge on them. Electric tea lights glow in votives along the mantle of the wood burning fireplace.

It's eleven thousand times nicer than my apartment back in the city. Or any placed I've lived my entire life.

"There's a TV." Zoey picks up one of the three remotes on the glass coffee table and presses a button. The landscape of Lake Michigan at sunrise descends into the wall, revealing a flatscreen. "Ciaran insisted on the size, and Declan found out how to mask it."

"That's amazing," I say. "Are you sure it's alright that I stay here?"

"Of course!" Zoey opens her arms wide. For a moment, I hesitate, then I step into them, feeling like twelve seconds have passed and not twelve years. She still smells like vanilla and hot morning coffee. Patting me on the back, she pulls me close to her. "It's just a shame Charlie is at that hotelier's conference in Portland. I know he'll be devastated that he didn't get to see you. He'll want to gush over your success."

"Tell him I miss him." I squeeze her once more before she lets me go. "He was always really nice to me." Charlie Foster, the patriarch of the family, used to make sure I did my homework at the end of the day, and had gotten me a job at a music shop in town.

What has my mom done for me? Exactly.

"Will do." Zoey turns her bright gaze toward Louise. "And Ms. Fields, is there anything we can do for you? A friend of Daughtry's is a friend of ours."

"Thank you, but I'm fine over at Serenity Bay. It's a good thing I booked early, the place is packed. Looking around here, you'll have the same problem. This cottage is gorgeous." Louise gestures with one smooth brown hand.

"Take this, at least." Zoey hands Louise a bottle of wine wrapped with a red bow. "We're proud of our wines here."

"Thank you." Louise glances down at the bottle and a shallow furrow forms between her brows. "Dumpster Fire Red Blend? Sounds...delicious."

"I know, it's a horrible name. My son names all the wines." Zoey grimaces. "He was going through a rough time. But give it a try. It's delightful. Very fruit forward, low tannins."

"I'll save it for a special occasion." Louise slips the bottle into her voluminous leather tote bag. "You all right, Daughtry? Need anything?"

"Nope. I'm all set." I lift my guitar case to prove it. "I'll be ready at nine on the dot tomorrow for the interview."

"Excellent." Louise flashes me a thumbs up before slinging her tote bag over her shoulder. "The car will be out front."

"We can drive her," Zoey says quickly. "If that would help at all. I have two very capable sons."

Don't I know that already?

"Up to Daughtry. Text me what you want. I'm off to try some of the local delicacies." Louise waves goodbye and leaves the cottage.

Like life is that easy. A simple text and all my desires

would be delivered. Out here, I can't even get pizza delivery five days of the week.

Zoey's pocket chirps, and she removes her phone. "I've got to go. I forgot about the floral delivery for the tasting room. Here. Let me send you my number." Two seconds later and my own phone buzzes in E flat. "You need anything at all, don't hesitate. When you're here, you're family." She pauses. "I'll work on that tagline. So happy to have you here, hon." With a quick squeeze, Zoey leaves, too.

I pause for a good ten seconds. The cottage is so quiet all of a sudden. I sink down onto the plush cream-colored couch.

What the hell do I do now?

This is all too nice, too luxurious. Suffocating, almost. It's too easy to fall back into the old habits of letting the Fosters take care of me. They aren't my family. They don't owe me anything, and yet I keep racking up debts to them.

Like the universe is listening, my phone rings. "One Way or Another," by Blondie. My stomach sinks. I've only labeled one person with that song.

It's better to answer. If I don't, she will keep calling or emailing until it's an endless ring of virtual toxicity. I steel my shoulders and swipe the bar to answer. "Hi, Mom."

"Daughtry babe! How are you?" Her voice sounds tinny, and there are bells jingling in the background. She is either at a casino or a children's indoor playground. Neither surprises me.

"Fine." I pick up one of the remote controls and push a button on it for fun. Smooth jazz plays from invisible speakers. I tap another button and the music shifts to eighties hair metal. That seems an apt accompaniment to this talk with my mom. Both things drive ice picks into my eyeballs.

"I'm in Atlantic City, and it's amazing. Roger—you remember Roger—took me for the weekend. How's LA?"

I do not remember Roger. Or Steve. Or Carson. Or any of the other nameless men she takes up with on a whim. "I imagine it's sunny."

"Oh right!" Hah. Like I believe that tone. That's the same tone she used when she called the night before my first album released, and she just "happened to forget." She asked for money then, too. "You're on tour. How's it going? Where are you?"

I debate lying, but there's no point. Wherever I am, it isn't near her, and that works for me. "Wisconsin."

"Wisconsin?" Her voice rises an octave. It's practically a screech. "Ugh. I never understood why you liked Wisconsin. So fucking cold. And the summers? Is it humid right now? I'll bet it's so humid the mosquitos stand in a big cloud to eat you alive. Atlantic City is gorgeous. The beach is right here."

She doesn't require a response. I leave her on speaker-phone and open up my guitar case. I always set a mental ten minute timer on calls with my mom. Otherwise, I end up in bed with a migraine, or a random hookup whose name I never ask.

We all have our vices.

"Anyway, you know it's been hard holding down a job. People are so ageist out here on the East Coast." This means she got fired from Target. Or Wawa. I lose track of which minimum wage job she holds at which time. She goes through them faster than she goes through men. It has nothing to do with ageism, either. Appropriately, most employers frown on employees who either show up hungover or completely skip shifts. "Roger's having it rough, too. Any chance you can float us until something new comes my way?"

At least she got to the point more quickly than usual. "I already send you something every month, Mom." Louise told me very clearly that I am not to indulge my mom's needy behavior. I'm supposed to have boundaries, stick to them, eat properly, and get enough sleep. I do...none of those things. "I don't have anything left over. I couldn't find a sublet while I'm on the road, so I'm paying rent in the sixth most expensive city in the world." Hopefully, once the tour starts, and I have some buzz behind my name, I'll have more money. That's the goal. In the meantime, though, I'm nickel and diming my life yet again.

There's something about not having money that leads me to make reckless decisions. Such as dying my hair with markers. Or getting a piercing from a friend who bought their equipment online from a discount store. Or staying with my ex-boyfriend's family in his too-nice-for-me guest cottage.

Mom scoffs. "Like it's more expensive than New York." Technically, she lives in New Jersey, unless she moved again and forgot to tell me. The first time *that* happened I was twelve and didn't find out until she neglected to pick me up after school. The parents of my only friend at the time, Maxine, had taken pity on me and let me stay at their house while the cops found my mom. Turns out she had run off for the weekend and married number four—no, number five— of my seven stepdads and was two states away in Kentucky.

I hated the seventh grade.

"Daughtry, please. We're blood, baby. You can't let blood down."

There's no use listing the ways she lets me down. "If I come into more money, I'll let you know. I have to go and practice, Mom. My set is tomorrow, and I have an interview to prepare for."

"An interview?" I can almost hear her ears perk up. "Say something nice about me. I love reading about how I helped my baby girl rise to stardom."

Ha. Hahahahahahahaha.

I inhale deeply and speak through gritted teeth. "Right. Sure. Bye, Mom."

"Bye, baby."

She hangs up before we reach the five minute mark. Good.

It's impossible to focus on anything right now. Music is a double-edged sword. It's something I love and want to do, but then it also has the potential to bring Mom back into my orbit. My knee jiggles and even my hair can't seem to settle. I can't get comfortable no matter what I do.

I open the dating app on my phone—fine, it's a hook up app—and it automatically adjusts to my location. Only two potential candidates of men looking for women. One is named Rove, a scruffy, older man I vaguely recognize, and the other is Ciaran.

Why isn't Declan on this app?

If I crane my head, I can see the driveway. Declan's car isn't back yet. What if he comes to the door, his hair hanging all sexy-tousled over his face? His blue eyes would be dark again, nearly the color of a bruise. What does he taste like? What would it feel like, to have his hands on me, all over me, touching all the places I need filled, even if it's only for a few moments?

My fingers itch with want.

I set down my guitar and jump up and down to shake the jitters from my body, and my phone buzzes with an incoming text from my mom.

Ugh. My mom doesn't belong in this lovely little guest cottage. It doesn't belong on the Fosters' land. I worked so hard to keep the two of them separate, to keep her from tainting this.

I never should have returned to St. Olaf.

CHAPTER 7

eclan

AFTER RELINQUISHING the festival wine tasting tent to one of our very capable wine gurus—a college student working with us for the summer—I hunt down Alex, and drive the pair of us back home.

I'm not sure if visitors to the tent wanted more wine or gossip. The whole afternoon, I slung both, and I'm done with it.

I thought my crush on Daughtry was a thing of the past, a college infatuation. But seeing her again? It crashes over me like a goddamn tsunami.

"Daughtry is so cool, Dad." Alex taps his fingers on the legs of his jeans. He still has a blot of cream puff in one corner of his mouth. When he was a toddler, I once found a bit of cream puff in his ear. Uffdah, sometimes I miss those days. "She said I should find her tomorrow before the show and she'll introduce me to the Vendetta. Isn't that so cool? Who else would do that for a kid?"

"You are a pretty special kid." I turn down the long drive leading to the vineyard. There is a smaller lane that goes to the tasting room bungalow, and vineyards and orchards in every other direction. Not that I look, but the drive to the guest cottage is past our garage. The lights are on, bathing it in cozy light. I wonder what Daughtry is wear—

No. No, I'm not.

"You have to say that because you're my dad."

"No. I have to tell you when you're being a turd because I'm your dad. There's no law that I have to tell you that you're special. You just are. Embrace it."

In the rearview mirror, I see Alex's eye roll, but it isn't as pronounced as it usually is. I must have gotten to him.

I park in my spot in the five car garage and Alex rolls out of the back seat. Literally.

"Dude, what are you doing?" I ask. Simone Biles, he is not.

Coming out of his tumble, he turns in a cartwheel in the driveway. "I have a lot of energy."

"No more cream puffs for you. Come on. Let's get you protein and something with nutrients in it." I unlock the front door, only to smell my mom's legendary chili.

"Yes!" Alex pumps his fist in the air. "Chili night! Grams, I want extra Fritos on mine."

"I know." My mom walks out of the kitchen, wiping her hands on a kitchen towel that she has stuck in the band of her apron. When my mom stops to rest, I still don't know. "I got a whole bag just for you, hon."

Perfect. From cream puffs to chips. I can't be bothered to care. Alex will grow up just fine.

Besides, I feel like shit warmed over. Mainlining red wine at noon on a hot summer's day is…unwise, to say the least. I spent the rest of the afternoon hydrating aggressively, but I still feel off. I'm more inclined to blame the wine than the reappearance of a certain pink-haired singer. She is still gorgeous, and it is entirely infuriating.

Pink? Who dyes their hair pink?

Goddesses, that's who.

"Go wash your hands before dinner," I tell Alex. He races off to do that before coating himself in salted chip crumbs.

My mom points the washcloth at me. "I need your help."

"With what?" I follow her into the kitchen. We repainted a year ago, and now it's a cool ivory color with pale blue-gray cabinets. The island dominating the center of the kitchen is made of dark wood and granite. The entire aesthetic is something my parents call "modern farmhouse."

"Groceries." She points to two reusable bags sitting on the kitchen table, which is set into the breakfast nook, with a bay window overlooking the backyard.

"Unpack them?" I move to the first and take out a bunch of bananas.

"No. Bring them over to Daughtry in the guest cottage. I feel so bad that there isn't any food in the fridge, and it's not like anywhere around here delivers reliably."

"Oh." My shoulders tense. "I don't know. Isn't that something Ciaran should do?"

Alex inherited his eye roll from my mom, only hers is ten thousand times harder to ignore.

"Please," she says. "I don't want him hitting on that poor girl. You do it. I put chili and fixings in there for her, too. I remember how much she always enjoyed coming over on chili nights."

So do I. After the first time, I made it a point to stay at my dorm on chili night. Watching Daughtry moan over my mom's food did very un-fraternal things to my inner self. My mom misinterpreted the whole thing. She changed her recipe repeatedly, thinking it was the food keeping me away.

On the flip side, the new recipe she developed while trying to lure me back to chili night is, quite simply, the best damn chili on the planet. It could lure extraterrestrial tourists and convince them not to lay waste to Earth.

Seriously. No more day drinking for me.

My mom picks up the bags of groceries and shoves them into my arms with a too-bright smile. "Go. Have fun. Don't worry about me and Alex."

"I'm just dropping off groceries. I'll be back in less than fifteen minutes."

Zoey Foster tsks. "Please. You cannot bring a lady dinner and then tell her to eat alone. Besides, I need to talk to Alex. We've had barely any one-on-one time all summer."

I sigh. My mom is not a person to cross, especially when I'm already hungover. "Whatever. Keep my bowl warm, and don't let him eat all the Fritos."

"Sure." She crosses her pointer and middle fingers over one another. "Scout's honor."

CHAPTER 8

 eclan

I KNOCK a second time and shift the bags of groceries to redistribute the weight. This is ridiculous. It's weird my mom asked me to do this, and even more outlandish that I agreed. We are all adults. Daughtry can get her own groceries. Maybe she doesn't even like chili any more. Maybe she doesn't—

The door opens, and Daughtry stands behind it, sniffling, her hazel eyes rimmed with red.

"Are you okay?" I ask. My instinct is to hold her, which is foolish because I'm laden with grocery bags. "What happened?"

"This?" She gestures at her nose and wipes at the wetness underneath her eyes. "It's nothing. No worries. I was just watching the first season of *Zoey's Extraordinary Playlist*. It really plays the heart strings."

"Oh." I glance inside the cabin at the TV wall, but the TV isn't even on. "I've never seen it."

"You're missing out." She sniffles again and points at the grocery bags. "What are those?"

"My mom thought you would starve." I shrug. "It's her thing. She made you chili."

"Yum!" She reaches for the bags, but I hold them back.

"Sorry. She will kill me if I don't deliver them inside. She would say it's the gentlemanly thing to do. On the off chance your arm breaks between here and the kitchen." This is technically true, but I can't leave her if she's been crying.

"You always were a gentleman. I'd hate to disappoint your mom." She holds the door wide open and I step through.

This is a massive mistake. She may have been here less than a few hours, but the entire cottage smells like her. Music still hangs in the air like smoke, and she's set up her guitar on one end of the couch. It looks like that spot has always been waiting for her instrument, and now it's complete.

I force my feet to move across the living room to the kitchen and I set the bags on the counter. Daughtry trails after me, barefoot. "How was the festival today?" she asks, easing back against the ledge of the square-shaped kitchen table.

"Good. Busy."

"I didn't know you still worked at the winery."

"It's the family business," I say simply. "Alex works there, too. Even though he's not supposed to serve anyone." I make a mental note to speak sharply with him about that little indiscretion.

Daughtry chews on her bottom lip. "He said you're a teacher now. You don't teach summer school or anything?"

"Summer school ended last week, and it's pretty bare-bones. Since the summer season is the busiest tourist-wise, I spend a lot of time helping out at the vineyard." I need to stop talking. Go away, verbal diarrhea, go away. I remove a mesh bag of apples and place them in the fridge.

"I like cold apples," she says softly. "Some people put them out on the counter, but I like them better when they're cold and crisp."

My gaze flicks to her, but she isn't looking at me or the fridge. Her attention is on her cuticles.

"Me, too." I put away the rest of the bag while she watches. Pasta in the cupboards, eggs in the fridge.

Her lips curl as I stow the milk. "Almond milk? Your mom remembered the kind of milk I like?"

I remember, too. "She's smart that way. I bet you drink oat milk now."

Her laugh is a bright tinkle, like it surprises her as much as me. "Why would you think that?"

"I don't know. Doesn't everyone in California drink oat milk?"

Daughtry rolls her eyes. "That's a weird stereotype. Honestly, I don't drink much milk at all. Except with cereal, and even then I don't eat it that often." She shrugs and the loose mauve sweater she wears slips off one shoulder. Holy balls, she has excellent clavicles. They aren't usually a feature I look for on a woman, but on Daughtry it's like she's flashed me her breasts.

With a box in my hand, I focus very, very carefully on which shelf this raspberry almond granola should go. "You used to love cereal," I say. "The more sugar the better."

"I can't believe you remember that." She sounds pleased, which makes the muscles between my shoulders unclench minutely. "I did, but when I was working my way up, sometimes it was the only thing I could afford. There were two weeks after I'd been fired from my barista job when all I ate was off-brand Lucky Charms. Dry. I can't even look at it now."

"I get that. I mean, not totally. I've never been that financially distressed, but grad school pays shit. Leftover shit. I swept the tasting room for loose change more often than I can remember. My mom's cooking saved me."

She crosses her arms over her chest, and the sweater dips another inch, almost exposing the top swell of her breast.

I close my eyes and remove a pot from the cupboard by the stove. "I'll heat up the chili for you."

"Thank you. You were always so thoughtful."

Right, that's me. The thoughtful brother, the safe brother, the down-to-earth boring brother who's a poor stand-in for Ciaran. I'm the brother who can never quite pull the one woman he's always wanted.

I turn on the electric stove and dump the container of chili into the pot. I need to get over myself. Daughtry's here for the festival, that's all. She doesn't need me creeping on her. I never told her how I felt back then, and that's for the best. I am a single dad. I have bigger things to worry about than getting my dick wet.

Though that's definitely the wrong train of thought, as my long-neglected cock seems determined to stare at Daughtry's lightly tanned skin and the curves visible beneath her top. She doesn't have tan lines. Does that mean she sunbathes topless?

No. I'm noping right out of that thought process.

I stir the chili as it heats up, perfuming the air with rich spice. "So, why were you crying?"

That's a good way to chase off all the wet dick thoughts.

Daughtry blanches but doesn't move. "What do you mean?"

I point at the wall with my wooden spoon. "Your TV's off. You weren't watching the show."

"I could have turned it off when you knocked. Or watched it on my phone. "

"Maybe." Pressing her might be entertaining, but I doubt it will lead anywhere. "But I don't think that's what happened."

Daughtry exhales loudly. The roots of her hair are blond, though the rest is streaked liberally with pink, and cut into a long, wavy style with asymmetric bangs. "Fine. It was my mom."

I wait, stirring the chili like that's my sole purpose in life. Should I get back to Alex? Yes. Is he having more fun with Grams letting him eat his way through the snack cupboard? Also yes. Besides, I like cooking with Daughtry. It feels...nice, domestic in a non-suffocating way.

"I don't know if you remember," she says. "Most people here probably don't remember my mom unless they frequented the Broken Lighthouse. She's...she's nothing like Zoey. Your mom, not the TV show character."

I know this about Daughtry's mother. So does my mom. It's why my parents never laid down rules about letting Daughtry sleep over, despite knowing that she and Ciaran were having sex. They stocked his room with condoms, made sure there was her favorite shampoo in the bathroom, and turned a blind eye. The only one of us who didn't realize that she stayed at our house because there was no one at hers was Ciaran.

"That really sucks." Leaving my spoon in the chili, I go to the cupboard and pull down a bowl for her.

"Yes, it does. And it's only gotten worse since she found out about the tour. Part of it is that I didn't tell her, so she lords that over me. Then there's the fact that any little success of mine, she wants to claim it. Is that fair, Declan? Shouldn't I own my success? I'm the one who put in the work, the hours, the blood and tears." Those tears now curl in the corner of her eyes.

There are many, many reasons why I shouldn't contemplate what I'm contemplating. I haven't talked to this woman in twelve years. We were, at best, tepid friends as I lusted after her from afar.

None of that matters. She is in distress.

Leaving the chili on the stove, I walk over to her and wrap my arms around her. It's instinct, really. She shudders against my chest, like an anxious dog finally finding a spot to rest. Unconsciously, I pull her closer. She fits so well, her cheek at the right height to rest against my neck.

"Declan." Looping her arms around me, she sighs against my skin. This is so much better than I could have imagined. Her soft body presses against mine, seeking comfort, something I can actually give her.

Oh. No.

Oh no. Oh no oh no oh no. No amount of Fibonacci sequence or complex organic chemistry compounds can stop my erection.

Her lips curl against my collarbone. "Something you want to say, Declan?"

Only that if a person can actually die from embarrassment, I'm about to leave poor Alex fatherless. I clear my throat, and force myself to step away from her. "I'm so sorry. It's been two years since my wife and I split up, and—you don't need to know this. I'm sorry. We were talking about you." This is why every woman prefers Ciaran. Ciaran doesn't get inappropriate erections. Ciaran doesn't then apologize for getting said inappropriate erection. He would have teased, flirted, joked, and then ended up in bed with her anyway.

Not me. There's no chance I will end up in bed with Daughtry, particularly not if I continue spouting nonsense.

"It's a nice distraction." She leans back against the counter and stretches in a feline and incredibly appealing way. When did she shift from forlorn to flirting? It's dizzying. I reel a little, feeling day drunk again. "I don't know anything about your wife. What happened?"

My own blindness. I stick to my script. "Why do you want to know?"

She shrugs, her shirt slipping another inch down her skin. Fuck me, she's gorgeous. My cock throbs, and I ignore it. "Distract me."

If anything is a mood killer, it's talking about one's ex. "Josie and I met in grad school. She was getting her masters in journalism. That's what she does. International photo-journalism."

"Wow. That sounds amazing."

"It is. She's been in the running for a Pulitzer and everything." It's far easier talking about Josie's accomplishments than the many, many confusing things swirling inside of me. "She's in Burundi right now, working on a documentary. She calls every three days to talk to Alex."

"So, what happened?" There's something in Daughtry's gaze and question that hold me rapt. I can't move if I wanted to.

I run my hand over my jaw, feeling the stubble begging to be shaved but I haven't gotten to yet. She doesn't need to know everything. No one knows everything that went down with me and Josie. I'll tell her the same lie I've told my mom. "At the end, we both realized we were good friends, but not really in love any more. I thought she would be happier without me."

Daughtry whistles, long and low. "Ouch. What about you?"

"What about me?"

"Were you happier?"

Am I? "I don't know. I don't want to be with someone who wants…something I can't be."

"Hmm." Daughtry moves a step toward me and traces her hand up the midline of my torso, her hand searing me through the fabric of my polo shirt. "What is it that you can't be?"

Her touch scrambles my mind like microwaves, but I know what she's asking and I'm not about to volunteer.

Ciaran. I couldn't be Ciaran.

"Bold," I say at last. "Carefree."

She glances up at me, licking her lips, and all rational thought takes a bullet train to Kyoto. "Have you never done anything spontaneous, Declan?"

Somehow she has crossed the room and is within touching distance. So close, yet never close enough. If I merely flex my palms, I can grab her hips, but I don't know how to narrow that chasm. "I find spontaneous confusing," I say.

Daughtry picks up my hands and wraps them around her waist. My cock seizes this opportunity like it's a dying man with a thousand dollars at a strip club.

"Daughtry, what are you doing?" I ask, or I think I do. It's difficult to think of anything as she presses herself against me, nuzzling into my neck.

"Confusing you," she replies. Then she takes my face in her hands, and kisses me.

CHAPTER 9

 *aughtry*

I DON'T EXPECT MUCH.

I've kissed plenty of people before. I've had a whole range of first kisses, from blah to brilliant. Most fall somewhere in the middle. Besides, this is Declan Foster. I knew him a hundred years ago, and we were barely acquaintances. Have I always thought he was hot? Sure. Of course. He is, objectively. Hot people rarely measure up in the sexy times department.

Yet.

From the moment we crash together, everything feels new. His mouth is warm and soft and pliant. He doesn't devour me or shower me in saliva, but takes his time. He savors my mouth, my lips, and when I press my tongue against his bottom lip, he tastes of mint and sweet, red currant wine. It's intoxicating and delicious and I want to spend hours like this, his arms around me, my mouth his.

"Is this okay?" he whispers against me.

Is this okay? It's everything. He chases away all the doubt and old hurts.

I glue my body to his, turn my head, and pull his tongue into my mouth. His groan is a whole-body action, his arms jerking to hold me closer.

I grin and catch my breath as I nip at the scruff of his jaw. This part of him is warm spice, like a mug of hot cinnamon tea on a cold winter's day. "Hell. Yes."

Something snaps in Declan. His hands clench on my hips, and the polite, intriguing kisses become something primal and erotic. My mouth and body are his to play with, and damn, that boy knows all the rules to the game.

In moments, he has me up on the counter, my legs wrapped around him, his hands buried deep in my hair. I grind my core against his hard length, pleasure sparkling behind my eyes.

This is far better than thinking about my mom.

"Is this really happening?" Declan says softly, his lips trailing kisses like burning embers down my neck.

"If you want it to." I take his earlobe gently between my teeth and tug, eliciting another deep groan from him that I feel all the way from my toes to my clit. "I'm all in if you are. You feel amazing." This appeals far more to me than wallowing in my mommy issues. A few moments, a little pleasure. Some people's drugs are alcohol, or nicotine. Mine is sex. It's the one escape I crave. A hook up and a goodbye.

He unleashes a deep, trembling moan. "I've wanted you for so long."

He has? Really? This isn't how my hookups normally go. The moment of confusion makes me want to pull back, but Declan is here and warm and his arms are strong around me. Like he cherishes me and doesn't want to let me go.

His kiss is feral and claiming and it chases away all those questions that tingle at the back of my mind.

Unfortunately, they keep creeping back in. Declan's wanted me for years? I thought he barely tolerated me back then, and it always made me sad. I liked being around him, but after the first few times he visited, he made himself scarce when I was at his house. Which I had been, probably too often.

No. I don't want to think about that. Not right now.

Declan is here, kissing me like I'm an eight thousand dollar dessert he wants to savor. Though he isn't pressuring me, his erection presses against my center, and I want more. If we just get on with it and have sex, I can erase all the pesky feelings churning inside me.

"Declan," I say, and he raises his gaze to mine, though it keeps straying to my lips, my breasts. His gaze is dark and inscrutable. I could drown in those eyes. The fact that I want to means I need to change this dynamic.

So I reach between us and palm his cock. His entire body shudders, but it gives me back some of the control that had slipped from my grasp. "I want you. Inside me. Will you do that?"

I rarely if ever come from P in V sex, but sometimes I want that full sensation, the desire, the wanting, more than the orgasm. That's all I need now. Pleasure. Touch. Someone wanting me for something I can give. It makes me feel powerful and in control. If only for a moment.

So much of my life is in freefall usually. Financial security is a joke. I don't have a wide ring of friends, since I like to keep to myself. It's easier to leave that way.

A drummer I picked up at a club once told me that if I wanted control, I should have chosen a different career path. Success in music has very little to do with situations that are within my power, and not having money makes it all more complicated.

I managed that situation by fucking that guy's mouth with my pussy and then leaving him, hard and wanting, in an alley.

Hey, he got to keep my panties so we all won.

Declan's jaw slackens and his forehead dips to mine, pulling me back to the moment. It's such an unexpectedly intimate gesture, making me feel warm and tingly. "Are you sure, Daughtry? I don't want to hurt you."

His sincerity makes it difficult to think, and every nerve on my body throbs with need. We have to get this over with. This entire experience is already heady and exciting and far better than I expected. There's no way sex will measure up, and I can cross him off as one more notch in my experience list. That Time I Fucked My Ex's Brother at His Mom's House.

And I want him. I want to be filled for a moment, to chase away all the fears and doubts, but more than that, I want *Declan*.

That scares the shit out of me.

"Yes," I say, nodding. "There are condoms and lube in my handbag. Condoms are a must, please. In the zippered pocket."

This is a good idea. Definitely. Just like that drummer, or any of the others over the years.

"We don't have to do this." Declan's voice is deep and sends shivers down my spine. He traces a line down the middle of my body, between my breasts, and south toward my core. "I won't lie. I want you. But I think it's too soon."

Why is this making me swoon? Typically, I meet a guy, things escalate, we have sex, and I go home alone. Why is everything about Declan making me want to stay, to reassure him?

Control. I need my control.

"Declan." I take his jaw in my hands, loving the feel of his stubble against my palm. "I want to be fucked. We don't need to analyze it. If it's too much, then fine. We can put it off another day." I rub my pelvis against his erection, and it sends delectable sparks of pleasure through me. "But I'm wet and you're hard. So if you're into this, let's do it."

"Okay." His cyan blue eyes darken, to the color of the lake during a summer storm.

All bets are off. He kisses me so hard I can barely stand up straight. Every lick and tug sends familiar pulses of desire through me. Instead of going for my tits, he pulls down my leggings, leaving them around my ankles. Cool air hits my skin, but I'm overheating from the inside out.

He scoops me off the counter then turns me around to face it, his chest against my back. "You want it like this, Daughtry?" His fingers trail through the triangle of curls covering my mound. I arch toward his hand, whimpering.

"Yes," I say.

He slides two fingers down, parting my lips, and he finds the rubbery nub of my clit surprisingly fast. He circles it slowly, and pleasure spirals through me. "You're wet and I'm hard." As if to punctuate it, he thrusts his hips forward against my ass, then slips his fingers deep inside me. Oh, hell yes. I moan at the delicious stretch. "Do you want me?"

"Yes."

He turns away for a moment, and I see him opening my purse. He is surprisingly polite about it, not rifling through like some guys would, but he seems determined only to look only where I gave him permission. He removes a condom in a foil packet and a small bottle of lube and turns to me.

But instead of taking off his pants, his gaze is fixed on my ass.

"You have the most perfect body," he says. He kneels

behind me, and I feel his lips against the round flesh of my backside. Then he nips at it, which makes me jump and giggle at the same time. "Sorry," he says, covering the spot with his hand and kneading my glute. "I couldn't resist."

"I like it," I confess. This is, so far, a lot more...fun than a lot of my other sexual encounters.

Weird.

I rest my arms on the counter as he unzips his pants. I hear the rip as he opens the condom packet, and hot, sticky anticipation floods me.

"I want to do everything you like." His warm hands circle me, one of them going straight to my center. Ohhh, yes, he used lube and his fingers slide into me like a hot knife through cold butter and it makes me curl and purr with pleasure.

"You're off to a good start," I manage to stay as he fucks me slowly with his hand. "But I want your cock, if you put the condom on."

Declan moves his hands to my hips and I can feel the tip of his sheathed cock at my entrance. "I did. I won't deny you anything, Daughtry. It's yours. Everything."

Good. I arch my back, taking him into me, and yes. Yes. I love being stretched open like this. So much of the time I feel empty, but not like this. Especially not when Declan's hands tighten on my hips and he thrusts into me, bottoming out in one fluid motion. Hells to the yes.

He stays there for an instant, not moving, his cock pulsing inside me. "Look at you taking my cock like a good girl."

Ooh. I like that. Even without him touching my clit, my body lights up like a Christmas tree at those words.

Then he starts thrusting, and all thoughts melt into sensation.

Declan can fuck. The way he holds me, his heat, his scent,

all while his cock strokes the innermost parts of me, it works on a whole different level.

Declan's mouth is the best surprise of all. He leans over my ear as he pushes into me. "You feel like wet, hot satin against me. Next time I want you to ride me, grinding that perfect little clit against me as I fill you up. Tell me what you like and I'll give you everything."

"This," I manage to say, though honestly it's difficult to talk when getting railed like this. "More of this." To my surprise, the orgasm is already building, and I want it. I'm ready to chase it down like a wolf with a rabbit.

One hand finds my clit and rubs it. "You're having trouble standing, Daughtry."

My legs are shaking so badly from the sudden rush of endorphins and other sex hormones that the only thing keeping me up is him. "Then do something about it."

So he does. With a strength I admire, he lifts my legs off the floor and wraps them around his waist. I notch my feet against his hard ass, and grip the edge of the counter for stability.

This is some acrobatic sexy times and holy fuck, it works for me. From this angle, every time he thrusts, he hits my G spot. Tiny sparks explode all through me when he rams his cock into me again and again.

I'm definitely going to check a box for a P in V orgasm.

"Say it again." Pleasure builds like a warm molasses flood from my core, rising up through my belly and my chest.

"Say what?" He asks through grunts.

"Call me good girl."

He leans over me, his chest against my back. I'm not any kind of aerial yoga goddess, but I suspect if I lifted my arms off the table, I would still be airborne in his embrace. "If you want me to call you a good girl again, you're going to have to earn it." A stroke, slow and measured. It's so not what I want, and I whimper. "You want me to say it?" His voice is hot against my ear. It feels like he's growling through my skin and deep into my body. "I'll say it when you squeeze around my cock, draining every drop from me as you follow your own pleasure as far as it leads you. Scream my name when you come and I'll call you good girl."

Oooh, daddy Declan, yes.

He punctuates that statement by pushing so deep inside me, he fills parts I didn't realize were empty. My body sings, calling out to him, pulling him deeper. The orgasm is *right there*, bright and shiny.

Two thrusts later, and I unspool. I clench around him, rising off the counter. He shifts to support me, his hands warm and strong, and that only makes the pleasure last longer. "Declan!" I cry out through wave after wave of the orgasm.

He holds me through it all, giving me what I need. As my body starts to relax, I tighten my muscles around him, just as he asked. I'll milk him all day for those sweet words.

"Good girl," he whispers into my ear. Then he flips me onto my back on the counter and fucks me until I come apart again, tears dripping from me like beads of pleasure. Then, as my second, smaller orgasm ebbs, he arches his spine and empties into the condom.

"Daughtry," he breathes, then collapses on top of me.

I feel hazy and light and something like complete, caught and supported between the hard, cold countertop and Declan's warm, strong body.

"Are you okay?" Declan asks, his cock softening inside me.

I don't want to move, don't think I can move. "What the fuck was that?" I giggle, then cover my mouth with the back of my hand.

Declan's face clouds. He pulls out of me and disposes of

the condom, wrapping it in a paper towel before chucking it in the trash. He pulls up his pants. "I'm so sorry. I don't know why I said—"

"Oh my gods, no!" I reach for him, grabbing the end of his polo shirt and tugging him down toward me for a kiss. "It was amazing." I kiss him again, letting my mouth linger, trying to sear the memory of him into me. "It was sneaky, incredible sex."

"Sneaky incredible?" He bends down and pulls my leggings and underwear up over my legs. Which is good because I'm completely boneless at the moment.

"Yes." I let him lift me off the counter and carry me to the couch. He lays me down gently and covers me with a throw. "I thought it would be a little quickie against the counter, but damn, you throw down."

I watch as he fills a glass with iced water, then takes down a bowl and fills it with chili. "I don't think I know what that means," he says. Moving to the fridge, he takes out the toppings his mom had packed into little containers.

"It means you are amazing at sex," I tell him, appreciating the blush that appears along his tanned neck. "Seriously. If I didn't have a one time policy—"

"You have a one time policy?" His gaze catches mine, and there is something bruised and aching inside it that makes me want to shrivel. He sets all the dishes on a tray and carries it over to the couch.

I struggle to sit up through the rush of emotions and post-orgasm hormones. "I mean, it's not like a hard and fast rule. Haha, hard and fast." Declan does not seem to find that funny. "Hey." I reach over and take his hand. "I'm sorry if I said the wrong thing. Thank you. Honestly. That was possibly the best sex I've ever had. You're incredible, Declan."

His expression softens, and something deep in my chest

flaps like a newborn baby bird. "So are you. It was…electrifying."

There is something warm in his gaze that makes me want to stay there forever. Like he sees who I really am, and likes her.

It's highly problematic.

I swallow, my mouth dry. "You should get back to the house," I say. "Your mom and Alex are probably wondering where you are."

"Right." His jaw tightens. "I'll go. Good night, Daughtry."

"Good night."

CHAPTER 10

 aughtry

TWO HOURS LATER, my body has finally recovered from its sex coma. I inhale the chili, shower, and wrap myself in warm pajamas. This cottage reminds me of all of the best things about the Fosters. It's comfortable and welcoming and filled with practical luxuries.

I turn off the lights, ready for bed since I have to perform tomorrow, when I hear a knock at the door.

Declan.

My entire body heats as I rush to the door.

When I open it, Ciaran stands there. He looks freshly showered, his blond hair slicked artfully into a wave. He's wearing a red and black St. Olaf Fire Department T-shirt, with the sleeves rolled up to accent his arm muscles. "Hey," he says. That voice when I was eighteen and desperate? Teenaged me would have grabbed him by the front of his shirt and had his pants off within ten seconds.

"What are you doing here?" I ask. I'm fully covered in a tee and loose sweatpants but I wish I had a blanket. My ancient Alabama Shakes shirt hangs off one shoulder. I adjust it to cover a little more skin.

Ciaran cracks that thousand-watt smile of his, the one that wouldn't be out of place on a movie star. "I know, I know, I should have come by right away. I had a shift at the grill then I was covering the fire station. I wanted to see you, the minute I heard you got into town."

"Really? Why?" I yawn.

His brow furrows momentarily before smoothing out again. "Come on, D. I thought we left things…open."

The day after graduation, I'd told him I was moving to New York and that he should stay in Wisconsin. It was nothing personal. Our time was through. And he'd agreed. Later that night at a graduation party, he hooked up with a girl from Appleton. I didn't care. The next day I was on an eastbound bus. "I'm pretty sure we just broke up. That's how I remember it."

He leans deeper against the jamb, like this is not going how he intended. "Can I come in? I'd like to talk."

"This isn't a good time. I have to go to sleep. I'm performing tomorrow." I yawn again for emphasis.

Ciaran sniffs the air. "Is that Mom's chili?"

I stiffen, my hand on the doorknob. "Yeah. Declan brought it over earlier. That was really thoughtful of your mom."

"That's Mom." Ciaran runs one hand through his hair, separating the strands. "You remember."

"I do." My voice is soft. It's impossible to forget.

"How's your mom?"

I swallow, but my throat is dry. "The same. I didn't think you remembered my mom." She remembers Ciaran. Probably because every time she met him, she hit on him.

"She was the worst." Ciaran exhales, resting his cheek against his bicep. "I always felt bad, dropping you back off at that house."

"I don't need your pity. It's twelve years too late."

"I'm sorry, I—"

"Whatever, Ciaran. Some of us win the family jackpot, and some of us don't."

Ciaran frowns, which seems to be an uncomfortable expression on him. "At least you didn't get Declan in your family."

At his name, I clench my thighs together. "Declan isn't all bad."

Ciaran scoffs. "He's such a fucking goody two-shoes. You didn't have to grow up in his shadow."

I wouldn't mind being in Declan's shadow again. It had worked out well for me earlier. "I would have liked siblings. Someone to share the family burdens with."

"Yeah?" Ciaran quirks his eyebrow up in a practiced motion. He rests both palms on the lintel of the door, looming in front of me. "You've grown up. You look damn fine, Daughtry. You were always gorgeous, but the years have been good to you."

I fix the shoulder of my T-shirt again. "You, too." It seems the kind thing to say.

"I tried to reach out a few times over the years," he says. "I know we broke up because we went to different colleges, but I always thought there was something real between us."

"There was." Need. I had needed him and his family. They were my safe haven and I had been willing to do anything to keep them for the heartbeat I had with them. "But that was then. A lot's happened since."

He leans closer, his eyes darkening as shadows fall across his face. "I always liked what a bad girl you are, Daughtry." His voice is pure gravel and heat, and if this were a different time, and I hadn't just had mind-blowing sex with his brother...maybe. Probably not, but maybe.

Also, this is not the first time I've been called bad girl, and I never minded it. Right now, though, it doesn't sit well with me.

"Can I come in, D?" Now his voice is soft and silken, a rope from the past winding around me.

I push it aside. "No, Ciaran. It's late. I need to go to sleep."

"That's cool, that's cool." He holds up his hands. "I'll see you at the festival in the mañana." He mispronounces the Spanish word and flashes that megawatt grin at me again, but to both of our surprise, it does absolutely nothing for me. "I look forward to talking with you tomorrow."

"Sure." My hand sits on the edge of the door, ready to close and lock it behind him.

"Hey, one more thing." He sticks his hands in his pockets and backs away, but it would be noticeable if I slam the door in his face.

"What is it?"

"Watch out for Declan."

The mere mention of his brother's name straightens my spine. "Why?"

"He's always had a thing for you. And he's not the best in relationships. He's not like us, you know?" He waves a hand between us.

"Yeah. I know." I dry swallow. I knew it back then, too, which is how I'd ended up with Ciaran in the first place. There's always been something a little frightening about Declan. He is all promises and hope I know I can't live up to.

"He's a decent guy, if you like that stuffy-nerdy thing he does." Ciaran's expression tells me he clearly doesn't care for it. "But he just doesn't *get* it. He falls hard and fast. It's how he ended up in that mess with his ex-wife. We need someone temporary, right? We're rolling stones."

"Exactly." The word sounds hollow and falls flat. The mention of Declan's ex chases away the last residual pleasure from my earlier sex hormones. "I really have to go."

"Right." There's something sincere in his expression. "Tomorrow, Daughtry." He waves once, then I close the door on this entire conversation.

Tomorrow. Life is always different tomorrow.

eclan

"Dad, can I buy Daughtry's album?"

I look up at Alex from where I'm buttering toast. Or, over-buttering the toast. No solitary slice of bread really needs a full quarter cup of softened butter. "What are you talking about?" I scrape half the butter onto an empty plate.

Today, Alex has on neon pink eyeshadow and some sort of sparkly lip balm that smells like fake strawberries. "Daughtry's album. I want to listen to it. Please?" He holds out my phone with her album already pulled up on the screen.

Daughtry looks fucking hot on that album cover, which does absolutely nothing to help my sleep deprived state. She wears a thin purple tank top that slings low over the curves of her breasts. Her hair is ashy blond on the cover, in long, sexy waves, and her eyes are painted with liner in the shape of feathers. She doesn't show her ass on the cover, but the memory of it last night is enough to get me hard again. Her ass is perfection, a Venn diagram of all the things I find attractive.

Call me good girl.

She looks like a sexy rock angel, and there is no way I'm going to be productive if I have to look at that photo any longer.

Adjusting myself as discreetly as possible, I hit the purchase button and hand my device back to Alex. "She needs a sweater for that cover."

"You are so old." Alex fits his headphones over his ears and takes his toast and copy of *The Misfits* to the kitchen table.

Right. Old. I'm too old for Daughtry, or at least too old for her one-time-only policy. Is that a normal thing? I am not the person to ask, and there is zero chance I'll talk to Ciaran about it. Besides, four years seems like a much smaller age gap in our thirties than when she was eighteen and I was twenty-two.

Of course, this is the same refrain that prevented me from getting more than one hour of tortured sleep the night before.

I pour myself a third cup of strong coffee and do ten jumping jacks. Perfect. Now I'm tired, horny, and out of breath.

"Hi, hon." My mom walks into the room looking bright and chipper as a chipmunk on speed. She kisses my cheek then bypasses me for the coffee machine. "Sleep well?"

"Sure thing." Lies. I took a shower after I got home, during which I tortured myself with thoughts of showering with naked Daughtry, then woke up at midnight with my cock aching. Then at four with the same issue. I've never masturbated three times in one night.

One time only. Really?

The second I kissed her, it felt like this beautiful symphony of inevitability. Like my whole life had spiraled hers until it dropped us together in that one moment. When I was deep inside her, feeling her fall apart around me, all I could think was how I wished that fucking Daughtry Sutcliffe was an Olympic sport. I'd quit my job and focus solely on practicing.

Sex with Josie had always been fun, but never like that. I definitely never said half the shit that had fallen out of my mouth with Daughtry. I don't even know where any of that came from.

But it was our one time.

My mom waves her hand in front of my face and I jump back to the present. "Earth to Declan. You okay?"

I snap to attention. "Yeah. All set for the day. The wine and stuff is in the truck already."

Alex lifts his headphones from his ears and stares directly at me. "Don't forget you promised that Daughtry could introduce me to the Vendetta today."

Shit. I completely forgot. "I don't know if she remembers." Keeping my distance from her is the one thought I have to prevent me from making an ass of myself and tracking her down.

"She will," Alex says simply, then puts his headphones back on and devours half his toast in one bite.

Mom sips her coffee. "Call me if you need help. I'll be over around four to take over the tent so you can enjoy yourself."

"Great. What's Ciaran up to?" I can see his SUV in the driveway, parked at an angle beside mine. It's going to be hell getting in the driver's side of my truck. I mentally bang the door against his SUV a few times, and a small feeling of satisfaction settles over me.

She shrugs. "He came in late last night. I haven't seen him

yet today, but I think he said something about the medical tent."

"Far be it for him to inform us of his plans. Is he ever going back to his own house?"

Mom shrugs. "I'll never kick either of my children out of this house. You moved home when you and Josie split to help me and your dad out, and I appreciate it. But we still want all of you to live your own lives. Maybe you should look at moving out, spreading your wings at some point."

An alarm pings on my phone. "We're late. Alex, let's go."

The next three minutes are a flurry of running to the bathroom, complaints he cannot find his shoes despite them being *right there under his backpack,* and me sloshing coffee all over myself.

Wonderful. There is no way I'm showing up at the festival with coffee stains all down my shirt.

I run to the laundry room. I remove my dirty Foster Family Vineyard polo and dump it in the hamper, then grab a fresh one from the stack.

Running back into the front hall, I slide the polo over my forearms and then freeze in my tracks.

Daughtry stands in the open front door beside my mom. Today she has on a rockabilly-style dress with large pink polka dots, black mesh gloves like a Madonna tribute, and gray chunky-heeled sandals with tarnished bronze buckles on them. Her pink hair is up in a messy bun, free tendrils escaping around her face. Her amused hazel eyes flick down my shirtless torso, a hint of a smile playing around her mouth.

And like the douchiest of douches, all I can think of is flipping up that skirt and calling her *good girl* again.

"Hon," my mom says, her expression all innocence. "Put a darn shirt on. Did I forget to mention that I volunteered you to drive Daughtry into town? We need good reviews, since she's our first guest, so you know we need to go the extra mile." She chuckles and elbows Daughtry, who smiles in a good-natured way. "Hah. Literally."

My hands are handcuffed by my polo shirt, or I might have strangled my beloved mother. "Sure. Town. No problem."

CHAPTER 12

 aughtry

DECLAN IS SNEAKY BUFF. I assumed, since he basically held me up while he fucked me last night, but I had no idea he was hiding a six pack behind those polo shirts. It's enough to make me tingle all over.

I've been tingling all night.

He drives along the streets of St. Olaf like if he glances away from the road, he might explode into a glitter volcano.

Alex, who is sitting in the backseat, taps me on my shoulder. "I like your music, Daughtry. Dad bought me your album. 'Chemistry' is my favorite so far."

I look back at him. "Mine, too. Love your eye shadow, by the way. That color is fab."

"Thanks. Dad takes me to Sephora and I can use my allowance to get whatever I want." Alex puts his headphones back on and rests in the backseat, humming along to my songs.

"That's the dream," I say, snuggling into the passenger seat.

"What do you mean?" His voice is deep, and all it does is remind me of him whispering all those naughty sexy things in my ear.

"Hearing my songs in the wild." If I look at his hands on the wheel, I picture those same hands on my body, holding me aloft. I've never been fucked so well or thoroughly before. He left me on that couch a limp pile of sated nerves. I couldn't even lift my spoon to eat the chili for a good fifteen minutes after he'd left, not that I was hungry for food. Declan Foster, sex god, and I made a promise to myself years ago not to dip my toes into the same pool twice.

Fuck it. Promises are made to be broken and turned into songs. Why not treat myself?

"What's it like being famous?" he asks, still not looking at me. Maybe last night was an every night occurrence for him, as he works his way through the female population of Door County.

I doubt that. Or maybe I just want it not to be true. I want to believe I'm special to him.

That is a dangerous wish, indeed.

"I'll let you know when I get there," I say.

It doesn't earn me a smile. He turns the car onto Cherry Lane and drives toward the library. "What are you doing in town?"

"I have an interview. My manager set it up for me. 'Small Town Girls Returns Home in Triumph.'" I flash my hand before me like the words are on a marquee. "It would sound less like bullshit if I were actually from here."

"Technically, you are." He parks in front of the library, where the interview is slated to occur. The newspaper is run out of a back office there.

"I guess I am more from St. Olaf than anywhere else. No one's ever really from LA. Prior to here, the longest we lived anywhere was with my mom's family in Nebraska, and that was only six months before she couldn't take it any more."

Declan is silent for a moment. He runs his fingers over the steering wheel. "What did you think of Nebraska?"

When my mom told me to pack up my suitcase—a drab little thing I never wanted to decorate because I preferred it forgettable—it was like she had punched me in the gut. My grandparents were more religious than I was used to, but I hadn't minded it. There had been hot food, chickens to feed, and a soft bed. They taught me how to play gin rummy without gambling.

I swallow. "I was twelve and so desperate to feel wanted I contemplated actually taking a bus back to their house once. Puberty sucks." I stick my thumb toward the back seat. "Sorry about that. I've heard it's rougher on parents than on kids."

"Alex is his own person. I think he'll be fine. We'll get through it."

I bite my lip, but then how would smeared lipstick look in front of the journalist? I flip down the mirror and dab on a little more lipstick. I feel the weight of Declan's gaze on me, but I resist the urge to see what color those eyes are now. "Does he talk to his mom a lot?"

"Alex? Yeah. Josie calls every few days, if not more often. And they email and text all the time. Josie wants him to stay with her in Chicago, when she gets back from Burundi. They have a great relationship."

That sets off an itch behind my eyes that I don't wish to explore without my full cosmetic case handy. "He's really lucky to have your family looking out for him."

Declan's jaw tightens and he stares out the window at

Maddy Olmstead, walking an enormous Labradoodle. She waves brightly at us. "You have people looking out for you, too, Daughtry."

The itch becomes more insistent. This is untenable.

I unbuckle my seatbelt and lean over the front seat to tap Alex on his knee. I do not miss how Declan's gaze snaps to the dip of my dress over my breasts. "Hey." Alex glances up. "If you still want to meet the Vendetta, you and your dad come find me around noon. We'll be over by the stage practicing."

His eyes, so like Declan's I'm not sure how I ever thought they might be Ciaran's, glow. "Definitely. We will definitely be there. Right, Dad?"

"Absolutely." Declan's gaze snaps from my legs to my face. "Good luck on your interview, Daughtry. You'll smash it."

"So, Daughtry," Helena Hartwell, the journalist, says, crossing her legs at the ankles and leaning forward. We are in a back reading room of the library, filled with thickly upholstered chairs, a fireplace, and little book nooks everywhere. "You have famously stated that you never go back to a place you've lived before. How does it feel, being back in St. Olaf?"

"St. Olaf was always my favorite growing up," I reply. Louise told me to minimize my mom drama as much as possible, and I'm damn sure going to try. "The people here are so welcoming, the county is gorgeous, and the food is off the charts good. Plus, now I'm over twenty-one so I can finally enjoy all the local brews and wines."

Helena smiles, but it doesn't reach her eyes. She's young, a graduate student who is moonlighting with the local paper. She looks hungry, which only puts me more on guard. "Tell us a little bit more about your upbringing. We talked with

Emma Larson, who went to high school with you, and she told us you were only here for senior year. It had to be difficult, bouncing from place to place."

My feet burn in sympathetic memory, but I promised Louise I would keep it polite. And vague. "I can see how it would come across like that. But I loved it. We saw the whole country, I met a ton of interesting people, and all of those experiences have really helped my music."

Her grin widens. Her skin is pale and freckled, and her dark brown eyes are wide-set. She's dressed today in a white button down and black slacks like this is an interview for a major news outlet, not the local paper that tends to run farm news on the front page. "Your songs are beautiful, and so heartfelt. Have you written any songs about your family?"

What would I have titled them? "Latchkey Kid at Five?" Yeah, that would've been a viral sensation.

I sip a glass of water. "I wrote one about my grandparents. 'Board Games.'"

Helena types a few words onto her tablet. Probably *"refuses to talk about her mom."* Or maybe, *She glances around the room that smells like Christmas morning, one Daughtry never got to have.*

Jeez, I'm maudlin today. One night of smoking hot sex with my ex's brother and I'm an emotional wet blanket.

"That one reminded me of my grandparents, too," Helena says softly. "We used to sit after dinner and play this ancient Monopoly set. All the cards were faded, but my brothers and I took turns coloring them in. Are you still in touch with your grandparents?"

"No," I say immediately, then realize it's the wrong thing to say. If that ends up in the interview, someone—*cough cough* my mom—will interpret that she kept them from me. "Unfortunately, they died about five years ago."

"Did you go back there for the funeral?"

I laugh, a harsh, brittle sound that reminds me of balloons popping. "No. I mean, I wasn't able to go. I wanted to. They died within six months of each other." My mom didn't tell me until three months after my grandmother had died, and only because I called her frantically, asking why I couldn't reach them.

"They must have loved each other, and you, a great deal."

"Yes," I say tightly.

If my grandparents had loved me, they would have fought harder for me. But that's the thing about me. No one fights to love me. And it's better that way. No regrets. Cut ties and move on. That way, I can't get hurt.

Right?

Helena pauses, as though waiting for me to continue. I merely sip my water, and she glances down at her tablet. She scrolls, as though finding her next question. At this rate, this interview is going to give me a cracked molar. Maybe the emergency dentist looks like Declan and will call me *good girl*.

I didn't know that was such a turn on. Maybe it's just that I've absorbed so much *bad girl* toxicity from my mom and men over the years who have used it to try to control me, being called *good girl* gives me my power back. I don't have to be what they say.

Helena clears her throat, drawing me back to the conversation. "'Chemistry' is so full of hope and potential. It's like that feeling of looking across a room at someone you're attracted to, and you see all the potential for a relationship. Can you talk a little about that song and how you came to write it?"

I swallow twice, but perhaps this is a better topic of conversation than my family or lack thereof. "I wrote that song when I was eighteen, actually. Right here in St. Olaf." Technically, I wrote it at the Fosters' kitchen table after I finished my homework. Zoey had made fresh chocolate chip oatmeal cookies. I thought I'd died and gone to heaven.

"Is it about a local boy then?" Her eyes sparkle with mischief. "I heard you dated Ciaran Foster your senior year. He's still single, you know, and considered one of town's most eligible bachelors."

Yup. I had stepped in it. "Yes. Ciaran and I did date in high school, and he's a wonderful guy." It's incredibly difficult to talk about Ciaran when all I can think about is his brother. Declan's hands on my body, Declan's voice in my ear, Declan's taste in my mouth.

What is he doing right now?

"Was it a difficult breakup?"

I snap back to the conversation and away from all the dirty memories that required an extra layer of concealer this morning. "I think it was fairly amicable. We were both going away to college in different states, and relationships are difficult to maintain when you're eighteen." Or at any age, in my case.

"First loves are difficult to get over." Her expression shifts, like she's remembering something pleasant. "If we look back over your time since then, you haven't had a long term relationship since Ciaran."

Uh oh. This is a quagmire I don't want to step in. "I don't really see how this is relevant to my music. I'm so excited to be at the festival this year, especially to be touring with the Vendetta now that they're back together."

"Exactly." She glances down at her notebook, like I just set her off course. Good. I don't want to delve into the many complicated reasons I stayed with Ciaran for so long, or why I now have a one time only policy. None of that is rock and roll. "Let's talk about your plans for the festival. You're singing tonight?"

I slip into the flow of conversation, matching her energy, all the while thinking about a certain high school chemistry teacher and what other secrets lie behind that gruff, sexy-nerdy dad vibe he has going on.

CHAPTER 13

 eclan

I'M GOING to have to rename the Dumpster Fire Red Blend next year. Though most everyone in town knows the story of me and Josie, all the tourists who are here for the festival keep demanding the innermost stories of my former marriage. It's all way too much.

As the pair of Gen Zers, who spent the entire tasting comparing selfies, leave the tasting table, Alex shows up, face smeared with vanilla cream.

"Another cream puff?" I sigh. "I gave you money for food. Actual food, with nutrients and vitamins and things that won't get me sent to parent jail."

"No one believes in parent jail any more." He taps the face of his Minecraft watch. "It's noon. Come on."

"Is it noon already?" I think it's a decent approximation of surprise. I've cut back to checking the time every eight minutes instead of every two. "Wow, look at that."

Alex rolls his eyes. "Seriously, Dad. Let's go. I don't want to miss this."

I think I have time to check my appearance in a mirror or with a selfie, but one glance at Alex tells me I don't. His expression is all pre-teen exasperation. "Right. I'm on it." It doesn't matter what I look like anyway. Daughtry has a one time only policy, after all.

I hide all the bottles beneath the table and set a little placard out saying that I'll be back in ten minutes.

"Let's go." We wind our way through the festival, which is thronged with people. Visitors shop, eat, or listen to the music from the big concert stage set up by the lake. Currently, there's a folk trio singing. They're pretty good, if a person doesn't mind their music with a hefty dose of twang.

"She said to meet her by the backstage entrance." Alex folds his hands together repeatedly. I haven't seen him so nervous since his first day of kindergarten when Josie and I dropped him off at school. I loop an arm around his shoulders and squeeze.

"It's okay. She'll be there." Hopefully.

The backstage entrance is little more than a rope fence off the side of the stage, guarded by a burly, overly tanned white man wearing an unironic crew cut and a black tee shirt with *Security* stamped on it.

"Hi." I lift my hand. "This is Alex Foster. We're here to see Daughtry Sutcliffe. She's expecting us."

The security officer harrumphs at the interruption. In his defense, we are distracting him from his Sudoku. He turns around to the performers and their entourages milling around the fenced area. "Daughtry?"

Her bright pink head pops up and she waves at us. Beside me, Alex's entire body grins.

Who am I kidding? Mine does, too.

"They're with me, Todd!" Daughtry calls.

Todd opens the rope gate and shoos us inside without another word.

"This is so cool," Alex whispers under his breath. "No one's going to believe this when school starts."

"Agreed." I've never been backstage at anything. The last concert I went to had been Summerfest in Milwaukee with Josie when Alex was four. It was nothing like this. People in summer weight suits stand around on their phones, artists sit with their instruments, and grips set up heavy pieces of equipment. Everyone chats and laughs or sings quietly to themselves.

Daughtry, in her gloves and dress and pink hair, fits in perfectly. Me, not so much.

It should not have irritated me as much as it does.

"Hi!" Daughtry glances up at me, her eyes sparkling, before wrapping Alex in a hug. "I'm so glad you guys came."

"Thank you so much for doing this," Alex says before I can even open my mouth. "You are the coolest."

"Thanks." She flips her hair over her shoulder, hitting me with a waft of her shampoo smell. That scent lingered on my hands last night after I—

"Hi, Daughtry." My voice cracks like I'm a thirteen-year-old again.

"Hey, Declan." Her mouth widens into a sinuous curve that unwinds all aspects of my composure. "Come this way." With her arm around Alex's shoulders, she guides us through the crowd to a quartet of shipping crates where four musicians sit. I recognize Ellery Vaughn from *America Sings!* Her guitar rests against her leg like she doesn't feel whole without it.

I get that. It's how I feel, with Daughtry here.

Ellery raises a hand. "Hi. You must be Alex and Declan. Nice to meet you. I'm Ellery."

Daughtry points around the circle. "This is Dante, Selene, and Lorraine. They're the Vendetta."

Alex vibrates with excitement beside me. "I am so excited to meet you guys. I'm a massive fan."

"Pull up a crate, friend." Dante gestures to the crate beside him and Alex perches on it. If he weren't nine, I'd check to ensure he's not having a heart attack. He looks stunned and mesmerized and nervous, all at once.

"You guys are my favorite band," Alex says, sitting on his hands. "I have so many questions for you."

"Fire away," Dante replies.

I've never seen my kid so excited. I owe this band the world's largest fruit and wine basket.

Daughtry takes a step backward until she's in line with me. "Looks like they'll be busy for a while," she says softly, like she wants only me to hear. That may also have been wishful thinking, but I'll take it. "I'm starving. Buy me lunch?"

My brain short-circuits, sending all sorts of mixed messages to my body, meaning I gyrate a little on the spot. There's a reason people do not consider me the dancer in the family.

"Lunch?"

"Yeah." She points to the food tents. "I haven't eaten all morning. Trust me, these are very good people and Alex is in excellent hands. You can leave him for a little bit."

Hmm. On one hand, I'm supposed to be working the winery tent. Plus, what about Alex? I can't leave him alone with people I've never met—music people, too. Not that music people are like carnies, though that might be an insult to carnies. Is it carnies now or carnival folk? I don't want to offend any one of them. Though come to think of it—

I'm getting off topic. Proximity to Daughtry scrambles my brain like an electromagnetic pulse.

"Alex," I call. He turns toward me, masking his annoyance. Good. It reminds me of my place in the world. I'm a parent. I'm an adult. I can control my life. "Daughtry and I are going to get something to eat. Is that okay?"

"Yeah, yeah." He waves a goodbye somewhere in my general vicinity then turns back to whatever Dante's saying.

"Don't worry, we'll take good care of him," Ellery says. "He'll be here in one piece when you get back from lunch."

Since Alex seems completely absorbed in meeting his idols, I absolve myself of my parental guilt and take Daughtry's arm. Her touch is electric against my skin.

"Let's get some lunch."

SHE DOESN'T HAVE any preference, so we wander the food tents until her nose informs her stomach what we will be eating.

"How did your interview go?" I ask, perusing the smoothie stand menu.

"Eh. It went okay. She kept asking me about my mom." Daughtry frowns and moves toward the pizza stand. If we walk much further, we will eventually hit the fire department grill, and I have zero interest in even the remotest possibility of running into Ciaran. I steer us past Laura Marshall's Sweet and Salty table, and pick up a cellophane bag of snickerdoodles for Alex.

"Why don't you want to talk about your mom?" I have several assumptions, but any little glimmer of her life that she's willing to offer, I want to hear.

She bites her lip and waits in line for shaken lemonade. "It's complicated. My mom was always on the move, always bad at relationships, always seeking the next best thing. I worry sometimes that I'm just like her."

She places her order for a strawberry lemonade, but I

intercept her reach for her credit card, and pay. "I don't think you're like her. I didn't know her well, but you're caring and compassionate and fun. Look how great you are with Alex. Nothing you've said about your mom implies she has any of those qualities."

Picking up her strawberry lemonade, she glances at me thoughtfully. "You don't know me that well, either."

I stick my hands in my pockets. "This is true. It's been twelve years. A person can change a lot."

She points her drink at my chest. "Or not. You seem exactly the same, only secretly buff. I'll bet you still drop all those fancy science terms of yours, and the ladies fall all over themselves."

"I have no idea how to respond to that." I watch as her lips close around her straw, my mouth going arid. "Thank you for thinking I'm secretly buff."

She elbows me playfully. "You're the one walking around your house shirtless."

"I spilled—never mind." There is no winning in this game.

"Don't be embarrassed. You looked hot."

"I looked hot? Meaning I do not currently look hot?" I ask. Bantering with Daughtry is almost as fun as having sex with her.

"Now you're fishing for compliments, which is never sexy."

I snort. "Very few people have ever called me sexy."

"That's because you don't pay attention." At my incredulous expression, Daughtry shrugs. We're moving further away from the food tents, but I don't particularly care. I want only to spend more time with her. "All those tutoring sessions? I kept trying to get your attention but you never looked up from your books."

My brain frizzes again like an old rabbit-eared television set. "Wait, what?"

"I liked you back then. But I thought you hated me."

"Hated you?" I pause, and she stops across from me. "No. Absolutely not. I never hated you."

"I thought you did. After those first few times, it seemed like you were never around. Even for holidays, you only spent time with me when absolutely necessary."

Something in her expression cuts me straight to my core. I've hurt her. I haven't meant to, but intentions are worth about as much as three-day-old dog poo. "Daughtry, I never hated you. I'm so sorry that I made you feel that way." She wavers, playing with the straw in her drink. It's time to come clean. "Honestly, I avoided you because I liked you. So much. It was difficult to think when I was around you. But you were with Ciaran." Saying my brother's name at that moment tastes like drinking straight banana ester.

Which, by the way, is revolting.

Daughtry tosses her lemonade into a nearby trash can, and lines her body up with mine. The nearness of her cancels out everything else. "I'm not with Ciaran now," she says, her voice like sandpaper on silk.

Alarm bells clang at full alert in my brain, but my hands flex and suddenly they're on her hips, my fingers rustling the fabric of her dress. "I thought you had a one-time policy."

"Rules are made to be broken." Winding her arms around my neck, she presses her chest into mine. So much for keeping it together. Her soft breasts press into my chest, and my cock hardens in anticipation.

This is every single dream I've ever had, barring my recurring nightmare about being attacked by the periodic table.

Privacy. We need privacy.

My brain tells me to pause, to think about my responsibilities. I left my son with a rock band. I'm supposed to be working.

But Daughtry overwhelms my rational brain.

I'm going to be spontaneous for once.

I step away from her and take her hand. "Let's go."

"Where are we going?" She giggles and stumbles. That won't do. We don't have time for her to injure herself. I scoop her up into my arms, the fabric of her dress rustling sensuously against my skin, and I carry her toward the parking lot.

"I can't do this in plain sight of my first grade teacher or my mom's friends," I say through gritted teeth.

She leans toward me and nips at my earlobe. "What is it that you want to do?"

CHAPTER 14

 aughtry

"THE LAST TIME I made out in a car, I wasn't this tall." Declan winces as his heads hit the roof of the SUV.

I pull him back down toward me and into a lingering kiss. I love messing up his hair, and sliding my fingers along his temples. The air conditioning in the car is a cool breeze against my legs. "You missed out."

He licks and kisses down my neck, sending pulses of warm pleasure through me. "I just missed out on you."

That sparks something deep inside me. When I was eighteen, I spent weeks dreaming of how to cross the line with Declan and not knowing how. Then everything happened with Ciaran, and I underestimated Declan's familial loyalty.

Which is a great quality. Not unlike his unusually talented tongue, currently tracing the line of my bodice as his hand slips up my thigh.

Declan has amazing hands. Have I missed out on twelve years of feeling these hands on my body?

That isn't something I want to contemplate, not as I shift to move his fingers closer to my core. "Say it again." I nip at his chin. "Call me good girl."

"What does my good girl want?" His voice is so low it strikes a very deep chord inside me that makes me shiver. Of course, that could also have been his hands playing around the seam of my panties.

"Everything," I say. "Your hands on me, in me. Make your good girl sing."

Oh, and he does. For all the women who say guitarists know how to fuck, they've clearly never banged a high school chemistry teacher. His thumb pulses on my clit as he strums every nerve inside me. The orgasm builds like a gospel chorus, and erupts in a quiet whimper.

"Good girl," he whispers, pulling me onto his lap and kissing me until breath is a faint memory. "I should have asked earlier, but are you on birth control?"

"Yes. I endured all the pain for an IUD but now I love it."

"Good." He nips at my earlobe. "Do you now have a two time policy?"

"No rules." My hands drop to his zipper and I palm his hard length through his pants, making him groan. Good. Now it's time for him to come undone. "It's a good thing you have a sunshield covering your windows, Mr. Foster. We are about to explore some sex ed that is NSFW."

"Unless you hid a condom in that gorgeous dress of yours, we're going to have to keep it to hands and mouth." As if to prove his point, he dips his fingers into me again, setting off more pulses of pleasure.

"I can make it work." I guide his hands toward my panties and together we pull them off my hips. I shimmy off his lap, kicking my panties under the front seat of his car. Kneeling on the floor covering—which is surprisingly comfortable, trust Declan to be so thoughtful— I unzip his pants and pull out his cock, which drips with pre-cum. I lean forward and lick his rubbery tip, letting the salty sweet taste of him linger on my tongue.

"Daughtry—" he moans.

"You can say no. Yes is also an option." With a firm grasp, I wrap my hand around his cock and pump him from his base to his tip.

His eyes drift closed as he groans again. "Yes. If you're really on board, yes."

Yes is the sexiest word in the English language. I lick the entire length of his cock, the hard muscle throbbing in my mouth. Within seconds of me taking him all the way to the back of my throat, he flexes his hips and thrusts his cock deeper.

I suck on the head of his cock then rock back on my heels. As fun as this is, I have other plans. "Let's do this."

Declan looks dazed, but he nods. "Whatever you want. I'm in, Daughtry. The whole Oregon Trail. Ride or die, until the wheels fall off or the oxen die from dehydration or we get dysentery."

"Don't talk about dysentery." I giggle and straddle his lap, lining his cock along my seam. Yes. He's hard and thick and hot and each time I stroke him, my clit tingles. This is almost better than penetration. "How's this, Mr. Teacher?"

"I'm the student here." He pulls me toward him in a bruising, all encompassing kiss that steals my breath.

That's the thing I didn't expect about Declan. He seems all buttoned up and strict, but he's so…passionate. It snuck up on me and now it's all I want.

Declan picks up a rhythm quickly, his hands gripping my hips and following me stroke for stroke. Fuck, this feels good. Not just the physical pleasure, but being with Declan, watching him take what he wants and get what he needs. A thick, vanilla-scented warmth spreads through my chest as pleasure builds and spirals in my center.

"Talk dirty to me," I say, my breath more of a pant. "Like last night."

He groans, withdrawing so he can stroke my clit with the dripping tip of his cock. "I fucking love your pussy. You taste like brandied cherries covered in the darkest chocolate. I want to memorize every inch of your body. It slays me that I haven't seen your tits yet. You are the most perfect woman, and I want to claim every part of you. I could barely function today, thinking about you.You want to talk chemistry? Your pussy clenching my cock is the fusion of two hydrogen atoms, setting off a thermonuclear reaction. We are covalent bonds, but nothing can break us apart."

I love those dirty, sweet words pouring out of him. I love his cock and the way he makes me feel. I love—

Declan groans, curling against my neck. "I'm going to soak your dress when I come, little rockstar. When you get up to perform, you'll still be marked by me."

That does it. The orgasm rips through me, like an atom splitting into millions of tiny particles. My vision shatters and sparks and it feels like I can see the entire expanse of the cosmos. It looks shockingly like a future with Declan, making pancakes on weekends, teaching Alex how to play guitar, laughing with them over board games and movie nights. Things I've never had. Declan makes me feel seen and smart and beautiful and kind. He makes me feel like I could be the kind of woman who can have these things. The kind of woman who stays.

He holds me close, not moving as I ride through the waves of pleasure. "I really am going to come, Daughtry. Do you want me to come on your dress?"

Through my hormonal fog, I dimly register his question.

On one hand, yes. I do want that. On the other, this is my big break and I can't have a giant semen stain on my dress.

Reluctant but determined, I slide off his lap and retrieve my panties from the floor. I dangle them in front of him. "I want you to come in these, and I want to watch."

So he does. I'll perform panty-less this evening, and it will be our little secret.

When he comes, crying out my name, instead of *Daughtry*, it sounds suspiciously like *I love you.*

CHAPTER 15

eclan

I DRIFT through the rest of the day in a fog. Picking up Alex is a breeze. He can not stop talking about the Vendetta. They've given him a T-shirt and a signed LP, so Alex attempts to convince me to order a record player on the internet. I mollify him by saying I'll talk to Moe at the hardware store and see if he can order one instead. We're a tight knit community that thrives on shopping small.

Otherwise, it's work, selling wine, chatting to my students' parents, and trying not to think of Daughtry.

Which is impossible because I have her panties, smelling of her arousal and filled with my come, wrapped in a handker-chief in my pocket. It's naughty and sexy and I fucking love it.

I love her. It's always been there, just below the surface, but the explosion of attraction between us tipped me over. I'm two heartbeats and one more sexual encounter away from taking Alex with me and we'll become roadies. Fuck school and convention.

I only want her.

My mom arrives at four o'clock, releasing me and Alex so we can go watch Daughtry's performance before the Vendetta goes on as the marquee act.

"Dad," Alex says as we wait in line for his dinner of bratwurst and fries. Festival food is a special event.

"What's up?" I peruse the menu. Nothing for me with onions or garlic. I have plans for after Alex goes to bed tonight.

"Do you like Daughtry?"

Like a skipping record, my attention snags and then snaps to my kid. "Sure. She's pretty cool." Well done. That sounds almost nonchalant. "I really like that she introduced you to your idols."

Alex shrugs and we move forward another step in line. "People say you shouldn't meet your idols, but the Vendetta lives up to their reputation. But don't avoid my question. I mean, do you *like* like Daughtry."

This is a minefield I've never explored with him. Josie keeps her dating life private from him as well. Neither of us wants to introduce him to someone unless it's a sure thing. He's been through enough in his nine years. Besides, look at Daughtry. Her mom was married no less than seven times, the shortest lasting barely two weeks.

It's not like I'm going to whisk Daughtry off to Vegas for a surprise elopement, though, honestly that doesn't sound all *that* bad.

In the span of the last two days, I feel just as strongly about her as I did twelve years ago. More, even, as I get to know her better. Maybe it's always been there, just under the surface, and I buried it under obligations and work. I know she's important to me, but who am I to her? An easy fuck? A checkmark on her experience list?

A kernel of doubt settles between my shoulders, but I shrug it off. "What would you think if I said yes?" I ask Alex, choosing my words with careful precision.

He tilts his head to the side, but he could just have been reading the chalkboard menu. Who knows why, since he's been ordering his bratwurst the same way since he turned five. "I think it would be cool. Daughtry's awesome, and you look happy. Not stressed. I think she mellows you out. You deserve not to look stressed."

Oh. The couple in front of us finishes ordering but I don't step up to the window. "I don't even know what it would look like, me and her. She lives in LA, and she's a singer. She travels all the time." An old anxiety knots behind my sternum. "What do I even offer someone like her?"

Pushing me aside, Alex places his order then holds out a hand for my credit card, which I give him with numb fingers. "You and Mom are always telling me that there are lots of different types of people and different types of families, and all of them are good and valid as long as there's love. I know you and Mom don't love each other any more in that way, but you still love each other like friends, so that makes us work. Why not make it work with Daughtry?"

This is all far too on the nose for a discussion with my nine-year-old. "Eat your bratwurst. We can't be late."

ON STAGE, Daughtry is stunning. She looks like Madonna and works the crowd like her, too.

I'm ninety-nine-point-nine percent sure I'm the only one who knows she's commando under that dress, and it twists my insides into a pleasant Tesla coil of energy.

"She's amazing!" Alex says, dancing his heart out to her

rousing anthem, "Call Me Lady."

She is. Like there's an electric current between us, she keeps finding me in the crowd, her eyes sparkling in the stage lights. Shimmying and dancing and playing her guitar like it's the only thing she ever wants to do. Watching her perform, it's clear that this is what she is meant to do. Daughtry has big things in her future.

"There you guys are." Ciaran claps me on the back and wrestles Alex into a hug. "I've been stuck at the grill all day." He smells like it too, ash and seared meat. He glances up at the stage, and a proprietary and very animal part of me roars inwardly. "She's gorgeous, isn't she?"

"Yeah, she is." I cross my arms over my chest, feeling my expression turn to stone. Why does Ciaran have to ruin this? No, he can't. Daughtry's with me. Twice. With luck on my side, a third time later tonight. She isn't into Ciaran any more. Was she ever? She almost admitted it before, that maybe she hadn't loved my brother.

None of this helps. Ciaran stares at the stage like he knows Daughtry is pantiless, too.

Why didn't I talk to her about any of this? Maybe because she only just came back to my life yesterday. It's too soon to be thinking about forever.

But dammit, that's how it all feels. Like we're on the precipice of a future that is so much greater than our pasts.

I picture it all so clearly. Daughtry writing songs in our living room, teaching Alex to play the guitar or helping him paint his nails. My mom and Daughtry going out for girls' nights. Alex and I globe-trotting with her on school holidays. Friday night fish fries down at the lake, sitting next to Daughtry while Alex plays with his friends.

It's a white picket fence kind of future, I know that. Is that what Daughtry wants?

She's a star on the rise. She doesn't need me holding her

back.

The stage lights dim and she plays a guitar riff that has everyone in the crowd cheering. The air fills with the scent of popcorn and fry oil and hops. "Good evening, St. Olaf!" she says into the microphone, and the crowd erupts with applause. "Thank you all so much for having me back here. I can't tell you how much this means to me. This was the only place that ever felt like home growing up." Her gaze softens, and she plays a lingering chord that hangs in the mist of evening humidity. "This song is about a boy, of course. Love lost, and love found." Her gaze flicks to me as she leans toward the mic and croons into it.

"Grape Crush" is a story, soft and slow during the verses, then upbeat anthem during the chorus. The verses she sings are about longing, staring across a crowded room, but you only see one face. The chorus insists that you just need to cross the line to have the one you want.

The knot in my chest loosens.

Yes. This is it. Isn't she as good as saying she chooses me? Only years of stoicism prevent me from storming the stage, wrapping her in my arms, and showing the entire Rock and Wine Festival exactly who this song is about.

Alex pumps his fist in the air. "Dad, this song is amazing!"

I nod, trying to keep my expression neutral while inwardly, I'm dancing right along with him. It's amazing. She's amazing. I can put my doubts aside.

Ciaran nudges me in the side. "You know, she wrote this song when we were together."

I spin on him so quickly Ciaran takes a step back. "What are you talking about?" Maybe it's more of an accusation. I can't really say.

"This song. I remember her writing it in her old note-book. She used to carry that thing everywhere. It had a rainbow on the cover, and I bought her a unicorn sticker for it." Ciaran shrugs. "She always told me the odds of making it in the music industry were the same as seeing a unicorn in the wild."

I'm hyperventilating. This can't be good. I remember that notebook, too. It was on the table the night I made her pancakes. Is it true? Are all of her songs about Ciaran?

Of course it's possible. Not just possible, but probable. If one looks at the scientific definition of accuracy vs precision, it's both precise and accurate to assume the songs are about Ciaran.

Fuck my life.

He shrugs. "I went to see her last night, after I got home. She looked so fucking cute in her pajamas. I think we might get back together."

He saw her last night? After she and I had sex? Why wouldn't she have told me today?

I know the answer, as much as I don't want to admit it.

I'm nothing to her. A fling. A two-time experience that might get lauded as a brief mention on her next album, but more than likely will fade to obscurity in the back of her mind. I'll always be second to my little brother, and a distant hum to her.

The music onstage turns into a torrent of tuneless sound.

"I have to go," I say.

Alex glances at me like I've completely lost my mind, and he's right. I have. "You can stay, Alex. If Ciaran can bring you home."

Alex looks between me and my brother, who merely shrugs like it's an everyday occurrence that I have a major life crisis. "No, it's okay. I'm tired. I'll go home with you, Dad."

Without looking at the stage one more time—I'm not strong enough for that—I loop my arm around Alex's shoulders and we head for the parking lot.

CHAPTER 16

aughtry

WHERE DID THEY GO?

One minute Alex and Declan were there, the next there's only Ciaran, who keeps waving at me.

I don't want it to throw me off. I don't need that.

I finish my set to more applause than I have the right to expect. Citing a fictional stomach ache, I evade Louise's questions and head back to my cottage at Foster Family Vineyards.

Have I done something wrong?

Ugh, no. This is exactly the spiral my mom goes down every time she breaks up with one of her husbands or boyfriends. I haven't done anything wrong. I haven't made or broken any promises. There's no way I'm going down that mental pathway to a hell of my own creation.

I'm not the type to mourn lovers. At best, I write a song about the experience. At worst, I forget them.

So I do all the usual things I do after an emotional performance.

I take a shower and only cry once. Soap gets in my eyes.

I put on my cozy leggings and oversized denim shirt. If I picture Declan peeling it open, that's my business.

I make pasta and don't eat it, only because I'm not hungry. Do I stare at the groceries Declan brought over, remembering how he pushed me up against the counter? No. That would be wallowing, and I absolutely, positively do not wallow.

Picking up my guitar, I play through a few songs, trying to lose myself in the music. Outside, night finally falls. The late summer sun put up a good fight, but everyone eventually has to go to bed. A car rolls down the driveway, and I watch as Zoey Foster gets out of the driver's seat and stretches her back.

Ten minutes later, the back door to the main house opens, spilling light across the yard. Declan in shadows saunters down the path to the wine tasting room.

Fury builds in my core and I wipe the tears from my eyes. How dare he be so casual when I'm over here, sleepless and definitely not pining? This isn't fair. It isn't right.

I slip on my sandals and leave the cabin. I'm not going to sit here all night wondering. I'm not drowning my sorrows in other men. Not this time.

I push open the door to the tasting room and all my resolve falls away.

Declan looks as heartsick as I feel. His handsome face with his crunchy line of jaw stubble is furrowed deeper than an eighty-year-old rancher who refuses to wear sunscreen. He looks up at me from where he's packing a box of wine bottles, and the raw hurt on his face is enough to melt me.

I rush toward him and leap into his waiting arms. They tighten around me, and the unfamiliar and intoxicating twin sensations of safety and security surround me. Declan's arms are the hug equivalent of warm, clean-smelling sheets straight from the dryer.

"What happened to you?" I whisper into his neck. "I was on stage and you were dancing with Alex. The next moment you were gone."

He holds me tighter, snuggling me. I could drown like this, happy in his scent. "I ran into Ciaran. He said some things…it brought up a lot of stuff for me."

"Ciaran?" What place does his brother have in this conversation?

"He told me he went to see you last night."

He doesn't say anything further, but I hear the subtle accusation behind it, and it fills me with ice. "He came over late last night, after you'd left. We talked for five minutes, ten tops." I pull out of his arms. "I'm not going to do the jealousy thing. I'm a singer. I talk to people all the time, and people flirt with me. I'm not going to apologize for that or deal with some toxic bullshit you fester with your brother."

Hanging his head, he leans back against the solid wooden bar. "I'm sorry. You're absolutely right. With Ciaran, everything is so complicated. It always feels like people choose him over me. Even Josie."

"What do you mean?"

He runs a hand through his hair, and it flops back across his face, recalcitrant. "I always thought Josie loved me. It turned out she wished I was my brother. That's why we got divorced. I loved her, but she was in love with Ciaran."

Uffdah. "I'm so sorry. That's awful. But it's not me. I'm not in love with Ciaran." Was I ever? "It's in the past." I palm his jaw, turning his face toward me. "I'm here with you. Until the wagon wheels fall off or we get dysentery. Remember?"

He doesn't laugh. "I don't know how this is going to work." He shifts, resting his hands on my waist. "I'm here, and you're a budding supernova. I couldn't make it work long distance with Josie, with her always on the move for months at a time."

"I don't know how to do this, either," I confess. I step between his legs. "But I want to try. We can take it moment by moment, minute by minute, hour by hour." Lacing my fingers through his, I lean against his firm, sturdy, secret buff chest. Saying these things out loud is a catharsis I haven't realized I need. Every word feels truer as I give it oxygen. "I've never done this before. But I think you're worth it."

He kisses me then, long and hard, and air is the last thing I crave.

Each time he kisses me, I'm transported back to twelve years ago at the grape crush. I'm the teenager desperate for his attention, desperate for him to cross that bridge and make a move. But if he had back then, we never would have made it. I know that. I was too fucked up, too young and flighty, and I would have broken him. Which is why I never crossed that bridge, either.

We have to be the people we are now for this to happen.

He kisses the shape of a heart along my collarbone, and I slide my hands through his thick hair. "You taste so good," he whispers. His erection presses against my thigh, and my pussy clenches with want.

"Lift me up," I command. With one hand squeezing my ass, he lifts me up and onto the counter, giving me ample room to grind myself against his hard length. Stars dance behind my eyes, spelling out his name.

He kisses me again, longer and deeper, his tongue probing my mouth. His every move, every gesture, is protective. Every inch of his body conveys his desire for me.

His fingers stumble on the buttons of my shirt, so I help him out by fisting the lapels and ripping it open. Buttons clatter around us like rice on a wedding day.

Still kissing me, his hand goes to my bare breast, and then he pulls away, surprise and pleasure and heat shifting across his face. "Holy fuck, you have a nipple ring?"

As if to prove to himself it's real, his fingers tighten on the little bejeweled barbell. The tug sends a delicious rope of pleasure spiraling through my body, and I unconsciously grind myself against his erection again.

"So what?" I whisper. I can't speak any louder, not when he tugs on it again, not with the heat in his expression, hot enough to burn. Fuck, I might come from this alone if he keeps playing with my nipple ring.

"I've never actually seen one in person." He twists it softly, the motion curling through me, and I moan, loud and long. "I'm sorry, does it hurt?"

"No, it feels incredible." Shamelessly, I arch my chest toward his hand. My clit aches for pressure, for friction, for *something* more. "Don't do that unless you're prepared to get me off."

A wicked grin spreads across his face. "That can be arranged. Can I lick it?"

Speech is for other times. My entire body feels flushed and furious. Without saying another word, I push my leggings down over my ass, exposing myself to him. "Please," I say.

His eyes twinkle, his pupils dilated with lust. "You want to touch yourself while I do it?"

Fuck. Yes. I don't feel self-conscious. Not with Declan. He makes me feel safe. Loved.

It's either that realization or the sensation of his mouth clamping over my nipple ring and suckling, playing with it with his tongue, rolling it in his mouth, that makes the orgasm rip through me faster than a hummingbird's wings can flap. I barely need to press my clit before I writhe beneath him.

He keeps suckling my nipple as I come, riding the waves of pleasure.

Loved. Yes. He makes me feel loved.

Maybe I'm not my mother. Maybe I don't have to run from people all the time. Maybe I can have this beautiful thing: a family, a place that's home and not just a crash pad.

I don't want a plethora of experiences. I only want this one. There's a reason real love writes millions of songs. I don't need everything, I only need him.

He is my epic love song.

I'm in love with him, and I don't have a single clue what to do about it.

CHAPTER 17

 *eclan*

WE MIGHT NOT HAVE A FUTURE, but we have a present, and everything in me wants her.

With her hands fisted in my hair, she moans as I kiss her through her orgasm. It isn't enough. I'm in love with her, desperately, wildly, and the thought that she might leave in the morning slashes through me. I need to do more. I have to give her a reason…if not to stay, to come back.

"Do you want a drink?" I say, my voice husky. Reluctantly I look up from her nipple ring—seriously, I'm ruined for other women after Daughtry—and into her face. Tears collect at the corners of her eyes, and I bolt upright. "Shit, Daughtry. Did I hurt you? I'm so sorry, I—"

"No, you didn't hurt me. It was wonderful." She wipes away the tears with the back of her hand. "Honestly, it's just the sex hormones. And I realized I'm leaving tomorrow, and it just all feels like a lot."

I pull her to a sitting position in front of me, and wrap my arms around her. Her head nestles just under my chin, and it all feels so right. Like I've been waiting for her my entire life, and now my body is saying, *good, let's get on with it already.*

I want to ask if she has to leave, if there's any way she could stay, but that's selfish. I know that. She has her career, and who am I?

A stepping stone. A tangle in her bedsheets. A footnote on her sheet music.

The thought of that riles me up, almost more than seeing her nipple ring.

Almost, because it's a fucking nipple ring adorning Daughtry's completely perfect-for-me breasts. Nothing else will ever compare.

Running my hand up the back of her shirt, I cradle her against me. I don't want to be forgettable. I want to imprint myself on her the way she has on me. "We'll have to make this time memorable, then."

She glances up at me, tears drying on her cheeks. "What did you have in mind?"

I lean over the bar and fetch a glass and a bottle of the rosé. "Have a drink with me." I pour the strawberry-pink liquid into the glass, not splashing a single drop. Years of working at the tasting room finally has a benefit. "It matches your hair."

"So it does." She goes to take the glass from me, but I hold it to my lips instead. The wine covers my tongue, filling my palate and my senses with its light, springy pop of flavor. She arches her eyebrow. "When is it my turn?"

I can't answer her with a mouth full of wine, so I set the glass down, place my hand on the back of her neck, and pull her toward me. We kiss, long and slow, and I let some of the wine in my mouth drip into hers. She moans as it spreads across her tongue, then again when I sweep my tongue through her mouth. Tasting her with the wine is a whole other level of sensation.

"More," she groans. She wiggles her hips, shuffling her leggings down her thighs and past her knees.

I would have given her everything, if she only asked. Instead, I take another small sip of wine, warming it in my mouth. Then I break away from her sweet, swollen lips, and press my kisses to her pussy instead. She arches into me, seeking more contact, panting with want.

I'm not going to rush this moment. She tastes heavenly, musky and sweet, the acidity in the wine cutting through to make her the most delicious dessert. I find her clit and clamp my lips around the nub of nerves, suckling and nipping.

"Fuck, yes, Declan," she whispers, grinding her pelvis against my mouth. Good. I want her to ride me. I want to fuck the memories of every other guy out of her, the way she has for me. "The only thing I don't like about this is I can't hear all those dirty words you whisper when you fuck me."

"I'm saving them for later." I guide two fingers into her channel, letting her warmth wrap around me and picturing the way it will feel when she surrounds my dick like this.

"How could I not love this?" She grips my hair and pulls my face further into her, then arches her hips, drawing my fingers deeper, where she wants them. I'm now her willing accomplice. It's fine. I have my plans. "You are unbelievable, Declan."

"Are you going to come for me, good girl?" I stroke the inner walls of her pussy, loving the way it makes her entire body shiver. "Are you getting cold? Can I warm you up?"

"You already are," she replies, her teeth chattering slightly. "Keep going."

I pull off my sweatshirt and lay it across her, then return to my ministrations on her pussy. Within moments, she writhes again, grasping at me, pulling at me, begging me for more. "I don't understand. I've never begged," she says, breathless.

"If I'm not making you beg, I'm doing it wrong." I curl my fingers and suck hard on her clit, and she bends nearly in half, coating me with her sweet juice. I am so in love with Daughtry Sutcliffe.

I don't wait for her to finish her orgasm. In one motion, I strip her leggings down her thighs and off one ankle. "Ready for me?"

"Yes. Condom?"

Right. Safety first. I dash to the counter. Ciaran keeps a box at the very back of the receipt cabinet. Only time he's ever been useful.

I return to her, only to find her splayed across the bar, legs wide and waiting, a sinfully wicked grin on her face. Her pink hair spreads across the countertop like an algae bloom, and I have never seen anything so beautiful.

"Don't keep me waiting," she says.

I unzip my pants and my cock practically leaps out, narrowly missing my zipper. I don't care. I step between her legs and sheathe myself as she watches, her tongue running across her lips. "I'll make the wait worth your while."

"Big talk—" but then her mouth opens in a round O of pleasure, as I lift one of her legs to rest on my shoulder. I slide into her in one smooth thrust. "Yes. Declan, yes."

I picture a million moments like this ahead of us. I wrap her other leg around my waist and slide deeper into her hot, wet pussy. "Yes," I repeat, thrusting slow and measured. "Yes to you, Daughtry. You want dirty talk?"

"Yes," she whimpers, closing her eyes and grasping for me. I lean down, letting her wrap her arms around me. She digs her fingertips into my back, marking me. I keep thrusting, making her feel exactly how much I care about her. "Declan, this feels so good."

"You feel so good." I lose myself in the slow, measured work of fucking Daughtry, the way I've always imagined. "This isn't the right time, and you want dirty talk, but here's the filthiest thing I can imagine. I want you, Daughtry. I always have. I want a future with you. I want to wake up with you in my arms. I want to make you pancakes, grilled cheese, and pasta. You gave me your panties earlier today? They've been in my pocket this whole time, reminding me how good you smell, how perfect you feel. When you're on the road, I want you to send me your panties once a week. Wear them when you're thinking of me, and I'll feel like I'm right next to you."

She moans and rakes her nails down my chest and back. "Yes. I don't know why I'm into that, but yes."

I lean over her, covering her with my body, pressing her leg backward. "Open up for me, good girl. Because I love you. Now and always. We aren't covalent bonds, we're atomic. You might not feel that way now, but I think you will one day. I'm going to spread you wide and fuck you until you see it."

"I do." She cries out, arching her pelvis into me, asking for more. I quicken my pace, thrusting harder and deeper. "Fuck, Dec, I think I might love you, too."

"I can work with that." My eyes cloud with lust as I drive into her, pounding her against the counter, losing myself in her cries of pleasure.

She digs her nails into my skin, using me as leverage to rub her clit against me. A few moments later, she cries out, squeezing around me as she comes for a third time.

As she clenches around me, I relax, sitting back and letting her milk my orgasm from me. I rub her clit in tight little circles as I release into her.

"Declan." She pants the words, but she looks wrecked and

spent, naked and splayed across the bar as she is. "Fuck yes, Declan. Definitely worth the wait."

This is the best I've ever felt. For once, I just know everything will be okay.

I CARRY her back to the cottage like a prince who has just rescued a damsel from a dragon. Not that Daughtry needs rescuing.

She needs love, and I can give that to her. My family, we're here for her. She only needs to believe it.

Propping her in the shower, I clean her gently, then towel her off and wrap her in the thick blankets of her bed. I fill her bedside glass with iced water and bring her a bowl of my mom's homemade vanilla ice cream with a peanut butter swirl.

"Stay with me," she whispers.

I only war with myself for a moment. Alex is fine. My mom is there in the house with him, and I have my phone with me if he needs anything. I want this moment with her, because it all feels too fragile, like a single feather caught in the wind.

CHAPTER 18

 aughtry

I WANT to write this in a song, waking up wound in clean-scented bed sheets, the mattress warm and indented from Declan's shape.

Of course the song would be better if Declan was actually still in bed.

I stretch, languorous and lithe, every muscle and nerve in my body tingling with satisfaction. Rules are made to be broken, as long as the one I break the rules with is worth it.

Did I tell him last night that I love him? I remember hearing him say it, pounding the words into me. I believe him. Declan doesn't lie.

Kitchen sounds and smells waft through the open doorway to the bedroom. When I turn to the nightstand to check the time on the digital clock, I see a tall, fresh glass of iced water with lemon in it. I swoon a little and sip it, letting the frosty hydration work its magic on my mood.

Footsteps pad toward me. Declan leans against the door-jamb wearing nothing but his black boxers. Hubba hubba, Sneaky Buff Teacher Guy. His mouth curves into a wicked grin that makes me tingle all over. "You're awake."

"Thanks for the water." I point to my half-filled glass. "Did you sleep okay?"

"Great, actually. It's been a while since I slept like that." With his thumb, he points at the kitchen. "Pancakes? They're almost ready. I made them in the shape of the solar system."

"Perfect." I think I purr. It's appropriate in this setting.

"Okay. Five minutes, and they're all yours. Coffee?"

"Tea. Please. With honey." I'm grinning like a fool and can't care less.

"You got it." He turns away, as if to go to the kitchen, then seems to reconsider because he marches toward me and kisses me so thoroughly, I die and am reborn. "This moment," he whispers into my ear. "This and every moment from now on, I choose you. But I have to go check the pancakes or else I might burn the cottage down."

"Fire safety, then." I swat at him and watch as he walks away, the taut muscles of his ass rolling beneath the fabric of his boxers.

I drain the glass of water then slide from the warm cocoon of bed. Time to get dressed. Louise will be picking me up in an hour. My hands still on the handle of my suitcase. Today I'm leaving St. Olaf. We're driving south to Milwaukee, Chicago, Kentucky.

But how can I leave when I finally feel like I belong?

My phone buzzes incessantly on the nightstand. I left it on vibrate while Declan rocked my world last night. I suppose I should answer. At the very least, it's a good distraction. No need to pack if I have to answer a phone call. I swipe to answer without looking at the caller ID.

"You are no daughter of mine," my mom hisses into my ear.

On a list of the ten shittiest ways to wake up, this ranks numbers one, two, three, and four, particularly since I'm still buzzing from Declan-related things. Despite the glass of water I've just drunk, my mouth goes dry and I crumple onto the bed. "Hello to you, too, Mom."

"I read the article. I knew you would never send it to me, but I set up news alerts on my phone."

I never taught her that, and want to murder whichever boy toy of the week had shown her that trick. My anger propels me upward and I bury myself in the closet, pulling out clothes for the day.

"How dare you say all those things about me? About your grandparents? They didn't give a fuck about you or me or anyone else. I was a good mother. I took care of you. You always had a roof over your head and food in your stomach. You made it seem like I was drunk all the time."

Alarm bells ring in my ears. Sometimes the food was three-week-old stale crackers and the roof was over a couch we shared at her friend's house. Otherwise, technically, she's correct. But why bring this up?

What exactly does this article say? "I didn't say that, Mom. The journalist must have twisted my words."

Mom scoffs so loudly, I almost feel a glob of spit land on my cheek. "You think we aren't exactly the same? The apple didn't fall far, Daughtry dear. You want to bad mouth my relationships? Ha. The only relationship you were in long enough to wet your feet was when you were screwing that Foster boy. And you only stayed with him because you liked his mom's milk and cookies." She says it like Zoey Foster makes them with anthrax. The entire conversation makes me feel like I've contracted anthrax, or maybe that rare brain on fire disorder. "You're a fraud and a cheat. You're a rolling stone just like me, and you'll end up exactly where I am. So don't act for a second like your shit doesn't stink."

I don't know if she hangs up. Her words fade into a dull hiss of vitriol that slice through my brain. My body buzzes with wave after wave after emotion.

What does that article say? I rush around the room, tossing clothes and toiletries into my suitcase, not even bothering to fold them. I won't leave anything behind. Nothing, except one pair of panties, will ever remember I was here in this perfect place, in this town, with these wonderful people.

"Hey," Declan says, walking into the room. "Pancakes are —Are you okay?"

My mom is right. She and I are exactly the same. Why I let myself believe one weekend of good sex would change me is a thought distortion of epic proportions.

I glance up at him from where I cram balled-up mesh tights into a corner of my suitcase. "I have to go."

"What? Why?" To his credit—probably because he's an adult and not a man-child like so many other guys I've banged, my mom is right god*damn* her—he doesn't rush or crowd me. "If you don't want pancakes—"

"I don't want pancakes." The futility of it all is overwhelming. I tug on my shoes and stuff my phone and charger into my handbag. I wrestle my suitcase from the bed and roll it into the living room. Through my tears, I can smell the breakfast he made. Fresh cut fruit looking like a bowl of fine jewelry. Veggie sausage patties, crisp and hot. A tower of golden brown pancakes and real maple syrup, the butter gleaming in a separate dish because he thought to take it out to soften. He hasn't made breakfast. He's made me a feast.

But I'm not a princess. I'm not perfect. At the end of the day, I am my mother's daughter.

"I'm really sorry. I thought I could do this, but I can't."

"What happened?" He follows me, still not crowding me,

even though what I want is for him to hold me and kiss me and tell me my mom spews packs and packs of lies. But the problem is that what she said doesn't ring like a lie inside of me. It smacks of cold, hard truth.

"You deserve better," I say. I pick up my guitar, letting its weight ground me. "I'm sorry for everything. You're wonderful. You'll find someone who isn't always halfway out the door." Someone who can take time to appreciate the effort he puts into everything. Someone who can keep promises to him.

"At least let me drive you."

"No. I'll call a cab."

Declan runs his hands through his hair. "There are no cabs. There's one guy and half the time he's too hungover to come when you call. He was at the beer and cider tents most of yesterday."

"I'll figure it out. Just let me go!" I practically scream, and that's shitty for my voice. I'm such a fuck up.

This is why I can't have nice things. Even when I want them so badly it aches.

I push open the door, feeling off balance, but I've done this before. I've walked blindly into the future with only my guitar in my hands and heartbreak songs tickling inside my brain.

To my luck, Ciaran is parked in the driveway, and has climbed halfway into his truck. For the first time in what feels like ages, he's actually wearing a shirt, a light blue St. Olaf Fire Department polo. "Hey, Daughtry," he calls.

"Can you give me a lift into town?"

Behind me, I feel Declan freeze in the doorway of the cottage. I know what I'm doing. It's cruel, but necessary. He needs me to hurt him this way or he'll come looking for me. And if he comes, I won't be strong enough to let him go.

Then I'll hurt him more.

Because that's where my mom and I are different. I have the strength to release the men I love from the toxicity of me.

Ciaran glances between me and Declan then shrugs. "Sure. Hop in."

I toss my bag and guitar case into the back seat and climb into the passenger side. I can't look at Declan or the main house. This is it. This is why I never looked back.

Ciaran climbs into the driver's seat. He takes one look at me and whistles, long and low. "Whatever happened, I'm glad it's not my fault." Then he turns the car down the driveway and I keep my gaze where it belongs.

The front windshield.

CHAPTER 19

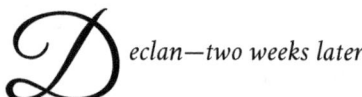 *eclan—two weeks later*

"DAD." Alex waves a hand in front of my face and I swat at it like a fly.

"Alex, I told you. I'm setting up my lesson plans." Which I should have done ages ago, but Daughtry's leaving hit me harder than a super flu. Her not responding to any of my texts or calls is the painful back to back whammy of getting norovirus and a broken leg at the same time. I'm an unmixed suspension of exhausted and heartbroken in a too-small test tube, but I still have to be a parent.

Joy.

"School starts tomorrow. You should be getting ready, too. Do you know where your backpack is? I'm not listening to fifteen minutes of you ransacking your room at seven thirty tomorrow morning when we need to leave."

"I found it two days ago." He taps on my skull. "Are you even processing in there?"

I ignore him and focus on my lesson plan spreadsheet. Who am I kidding? Will anyone give a fuck if I phone it in for the first few weeks? Ninety seven percent of the kids I teach will never remember anything I say.

"OMG, Dad, you're spiraling again. Pay attention."

"I'm not spiraling," I grumble, turning to Alex. He has his music player and headphones in one hand. "What is it you need?"

"I don't think Daughtry's songs are about Uncle Ciaran."

I sigh aloud, earning me an eye roll. "I don't want to talk about this."

"But you have to!" Alex thrusts his music player at me. "Just listen."

I don't want to. I can't. For the first week after she left, all I did was listen to her music and leave her panicked voice memos, none of which she returned. Week number two meant I formally avoided my heartache and any mention of its cause. "Daughtry left. She was here for less than a minute. Why is this a big deal?"

"Because she made you happy, and you deserve to be happy, and now you're miserable, and even Mom thinks you should do something about it."

"You told your mom about this?"

"Of course. I tell Mom everything."

Of course he does. "Why does she care?"

"Because she does." Things are so simple for nine year olds. All he needs is some pseudo-Greek mythology and a few magic wands, and Alex is right at home. "Please. Just listen to the songs."

"I've heard the songs. I've read the interview." The interview in which she essentially admits that Ciaran is the one who got away. The songs about how funny and special my brother is. It's almost enough to make me want to move out of the fucking house. Or force Ciaran to return to his own.

"You hear, but you don't listen." Alex unplugs the headphones and taps a button on his music player. Daughtry's voice filters through the speakers, and even though it's a recording, my body's reaction is immediate. It's almost like I can smell her again. I threw out the panties. No way I want to hold on to them when I can't be with her.

"Isoamyl acetate, watch me move, I'll watch you wake..." Daughtry's voice is clear and strong and gorgeous.

Alex hits the stop button. "Did you hear it?"

"She sounds amazing." I glance at the square-shaped photo of her on the screen and a thousand things shatter into fractals in my body. "She still needs to wear a sweater for these photos."

"Ugh, Dad! She says 'isoamyl acetate.' That's banana ester, right?"

Pride surges within me, and I crush him into a hug. "I can't believe you know that. I could die happy right now."

"You're completely missing the point." Alex wrestles himself out of my grasp. "Didn't you hear what she said? She talks about you tutoring her. That's what the entire 'Chemistry' song is about, how she wishes you would look up and see her."

That gives me pause. That can't be right. Can it?

But Alex isn't done. "And then in 'Heartbreak,' she sits there eating pancakes and thinking about the one who got away. 'Grape Crush?' She talks about how she dances only for one guy. It wasn't Uncle Ciaran, it was you the whole time." He claps his hands in triumph. That's my son, a self-satisfied Sherlock Holmes. "That is why we have to go see her. So you can get her back."

I hold up my hands. "That doesn't happen in real life, Alex. There's no getting her back. It's not like we were together—"

A hand taps me sharply on my shoulder. "Declan Foster, do not lie to your child," Mom says, walking past me and standing protectively behind Alex. "Of course you were together. Why do you think I kept asking you to do things, like drive her places, or bring her groceries? Heck, I even asked Maddy Olmstead to pretend she had rented out her apartment to someone else, just to get Daughtry here. She's a grown woman, of course she could have done those things herself, but I've always known how you felt about her."

That's an awful lot of confessions when my ears are ringing from her rebuke. "But, Mom—"

"Please. You think I really believed that you were just over my chili? I'm your mother. I could see the way you two looked at each other. You were right at the time not to make your move, but for Cripes sake, you're both in your thirties. Get over it and at least call her."

Like that thought hasn't occurred to me on average a thousand times a minute since she walked out the door. "I don't even know where she is."

My mom rolls her eyes and shows me her phone screen, where there's a photo of Daughtry singing on stage. "Nashville. They're only there until tomorrow night, so you'd better get going."

"I have school—"

My mom huffs. "You can miss one day of school in your entire life. Pack a bag and go get her."

"I'm coming, too." Alex disappears before I can stop him. "I've already packed your bag, Dad!" He calls down the hallway.

Perfect. Now I understand what it feels like to be ganged up on. "This is not some zany road trip comedy, Mom."

She pats me on the shoulder. "Yes, it is. By the way, Ciaran is driving you to the airport. You two need to talk."

· · ·

SINCE I HAVE ABSOLUTELY no say in the matter, fifteen minutes later Alex and I are in Ciaran's car with plane tickets my mom purchased.

"So, you have a layover?" Ciaran asks, focused on traveling the roads through our little peninsula.

"Yeah. Due to the vagaries of air travel, it's in Atlanta. So we fly past Nashville, and then back." I shake my head in bewilderment. "I have no idea how this does not negatively impact my carbon footprint."

"It totally does. You can't get off the hook for that. But then again, you're doing it for love. Go you, man." He punches me in the arm, a little harder than he has to.

I rub the muscle. "You're not upset?"

"About Daughtry? No. We had our time. Honestly, I think even back then I knew how you two felt about each other. But since I was eighteen and a hormonal idiot, I didn't know how to deal so I just ignored it." He shrugs. "I've grown since then."

"Sure you have." I punch him back, for the sake of retribution.

Ciaran glances into the rearview mirror, and I follow his gaze. Alex stares out the window with his headphones in place, no eye makeup today but he wears teal and neon pink nail polish. It looks awesome.

"Look, Declan," Ciaran says, not making eye contact with me. As his older brother, I know none of this can be good. The last time I saw Ciaran's confession face, he told me he'd "accidentally" stolen my car and then "accidentally" drove it into the lake. "About Josie."

Oh. Right. "What about her?"

"I promise you, I never flirted with her or anything. She reached out to me after your divorce, but I told her I didn't feel that way about her. I tried to let her down easy. I'm sorry." He turns to look at me, but there's a tractor driving ten miles an hour down the road, so I smack his hands and he pays attention to the road again. "I really am. I don't ever want to be in the middle of your relationships. You're the greatest, and you deserve someone who sees that. Like Daughtry."

Hmm. I don't like forgiving Ciaran. I never quite forgave him for the Car Meets Lake incident, either. But maybe in this one instance, I can yield a little. My marriage ending wasn't really his fault. Ciaran was a metaphor for Josie, a possibility that something could be better. I feel bad for her, that he didn't reciprocate her feelings, but I'm also really proud of her. She went after happiness, even though it was difficult. Even though she didn't know it would work out.

And it has. Josie is still in our lives. Alex is a great kid, and he has an entire network of people who love him.

He'll have one more if I can do this and get Daughtry back. Josie was right. We can both have something more, but only if I'm brave enough to fight for it.

"Do you need me to pull over?" Ciaran asks. "You look like you're going to throw up."

"I'm not going to throw up," I snap. "I was just thinking. About Josie and Daughtry."

Ciaran snorts. "Those two are going to get on like gang-busters. You have a *type*, man."

"Oh, do I?"

"Yeah. Smart, cool women who are way hotter than you will ever be. Or than you deserve." His eyes twinkle, the way they always do when he's being a jackass. Still, he's my brother, and I suppose some part of me—deep, deep, *deep* down—loves that about him.

It doesn't fix everything that's broken in our relationship, but it's an opening salvo.

I sniff twice. This is the most honest conversation I've ever had with my brother, and it makes me hella uncomfortable. "Thanks. Now can we please talk about something else? My ovaries are starting to ache."

CHAPTER 20

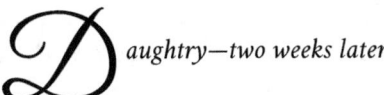 *aughtry—two weeks later*

"FOR THE LOVE of the gods, stop playing that song and have a drink with me." Louise sinks into the armchair across from me and sighs loudly. "What are you even calling that song?"

I set down my guitar. We sit in the artist's area of the recording studio in Nashville. First of all, this place is ten thousand leagues nicer than the place where I recorded my first single. Second of all, yes, the song I'm working on is not an upbeat, toe-tappy hit. Some might say maudlin or moody or Morrissey-inspired.

I don't give a shit what people might say.

"I thought I might call it 'Fall Out,'" I reply.

From her tote bag, Louise pulls out two plastic cups and a bottle of Foster Family Vineyards' Dumpster Fire Red Blend. My heart sinks lower.

"I'm not that thirsty," I say. Understatement. I'm starving, desperate, just not for food or drink.

Louise shakes her head. She went to the hairdressers in Chicago, so her hair is now a gorgeous mass of tight curls.

My hair, on the other hand? The pink is growing out, leaving me with bland ashy roots, but I also haven't been conditioning properly, so it's brittle and crunchy.

I have no desire to change the situation. It looks fine when it's up in a bun onstage. And disheveled is a totally rock-and-roll look.

Louise sighs and leans forward, resting her elbows on her thighs. She wears a fitted royal blue sheath dress, but it's long enough to cover her knees. "Talk to me."

"There's nothing to talk about."

Shaking her head, Louise picks up the bottle of wine and unscrews the twist-off cap. "I have to say, I admire Wisconsin wineries. It's such a pain in the ass to find a corkscrew when you just want a drink. Is cork even environmentally sustainable? Not to mention the ease of re-capping it later. Genius."

"I suppose." Her statement doesn't really seem to require an actual response.

I wait, my hands turning numb on the bridge of my guitar. Over the last two weeks, the only time I've felt anything was when I was singing.

Louise finishes pouring, recaps the bottle, and places it back into her tote bag. Then she hands a plastic cup to me. "Spill."

"There's nothing to say." Not knowing what else to do, I sip the wine, but it's the wrong move. It's like being transported back to the Fosters' dinner table, Zoey with a lasagna in her hands, the scent of the hydrangeas outside wafting in through the window. The wine is sweet and full of red fruit, with a pleasant, mellow vanilla taste that lingers.

It reminds me of Declan. His sweetness, his depth. The way he made me feel, cozy and secure.

Fuck it. *Everything* reminds me of Declan.

Tears collect at the corners of my eyes, but I wipe them away.

Louise sits back in the armchair and crosses her legs. "There's more to say. You've been moping since we left St. Olaf. The songs you've been writing haven't had your edge." She sips the wine. "Ellery and the Vendetta? They're worried about you, too."

"No one needs to worry about me." I sniff and set the guitar back in its case. "I'll be fine. I'm sorry if I've been off my game."

Louise holds up a single finger. "Don't apologize. Own your feelings. As your manager, I will accept nothing less."

This is why everyone loves Louise.

"Now." Louise settles back into the armchair, cradling her plastic cup of wine. "Tell me what your mom did. And don't ask how I know. It's my job to know."

It's a good thing I'm a musician instead of an actress, because apparently I've been doing a terrible job of faking being okay. Sipping my wine again, I use the flavors to make me feel stronger. "My mom did nothing except give me her DNA. I'm not sending her more money."

"Daughtry. You are not your mother. You are driven and talented and passionate. What you do in your free time is your business, but do not think for one second that because your mom was a terrible parent that you are the same as she is."

"But I am." My voice cracks and I make a mental note to switch from wine to lemon tea with honey. Otherwise, I'll never finish my maudlin, moody, Morrissey-inspired album. "I can't handle responsibility. I go through bed partners at an alarming rate. My feet are constantly in motion."

Louise finishes her plastic cup of wine. I suspect she put a lot less in her glass than she gave me. "I'm not going to de-program you from a lifetime of maternal gaslighting in one session, and we have an album to start. You need to call her and break up with her. Now."

"Okay." She's right, of course. "I will." It will be rough but not as difficult as continuing to avoid all these emotions. I'll be lighter once I tell my mom off once and for all.

"Here's the deal." Louise holds up her fingers and starts ticking things off on them. "You haven't been the same since we left St. Olaf. I'm not blind. Something happened between you and that guy from the wine tasting booth. The hot one with the cool kid who wants to be a Vendetta roadie when he grows up."

The memory of Declan washes over me, the naughty words he spoke ringing in my ears. *This is the dirtiest thing I can imagine. Waking up next to you and making you pancakes on weekends.* Tears pool inside me like a tangle of unwritten notes.

"He's a chemistry teacher," I say softly, staring into my wine. For a red blend in a plastic cup, it has excellent legs.

"That's wonderful." Louise's tone softens. Despite our minimal age gap, she has a vaguely maternal way about her at times that I find very soothing. Go figure. "What's his name?"

I pause for a long moment. "Declan. Alex is his son, the one who loves the Vendetta. Nine years old. He's such a cool kid, and Declan is such a good dad, and his family is just..." There aren't words really, for how I feel about the Fosters.

Louise purses her lips, looking remarkably like a therapist. Some part of me dimly recalls that she got her bachelors degree in psychology at one of the Ivy League universities. She's putting it to good use. "It sounds like he has what you've always wanted."

When she says it, everything clicks into place. Yes. That's what I've always wanted. Zoey Foster fussing over me or noticing when I change my hair. Alex and I dancing in their

—no, *our*— living room. Long dinners filled with laughter and good-natured banter.

And Declan. Declan, morning, noon, and night. Kissing him on the cheek in the morning before he leaves for school. Feeling his arms around me when I get back from tour. Minutes and hours and days and years of Declan.

A future.

A possible future, anyway. One maybe I could have had if I hadn't run away.

The realization strikes me like a fire tornado. I'm not my mom. I don't have to make the same choices she does. I have the power to choose my own destiny. I've *been* choosing my own destiny since I graduated high school. Despite the years of traipsing across the country, searching for my home, I know where I belong now. Where I've always belonged.

My mom and her choices messed up my childhood. I will not let her mess up my future.

I swallow, feeling a hard knot of saliva moving down my throat. "You are an excellent manager, and the smartest woman I've ever met, Louise."

With a mysterious smile, Louise stands and gathers her tote bag over one shoulder. "I am aware. So you know, after Nashville we have two days free until we need to be in Denver. If there's anything you need to do." She pats my back gently. "Now get back to that song. Maybe make it a love song."

I'll do more than that.

eclan

Six hours of flying and layovers and shitty airplane food later, Alex and I arrive in Nashville. "Do you think we're late?" I ask.

"It's fine, Dad." Alex stares out the window and yawns. It has been a long day.

I ruffle his hair and lift his backpack from his shoulders. I secure it to our carry-on suitcase. "Do you want to go to the hotel first? We don't have to go see Daughtry right now."

Alex shrugs as we wait in the taxi line. "That's the whole reason we came. Don't chicken out now, Dad."

"I'm not chickening out." I am. I definitely am. All the hours of inhaling other passengers' B.O. have only made me rethink this grand plan of my mom's.

And convinced me that I need a shower before I see Daughtry.

"Do they even allow suitcases in music clubs?" We step

forward but there are still five people ahead of us in the taxi line. "I have no idea what to say to her."

Alex rolls his eyes, which makes him seem more himself. "Tell her more of your chemistry puns. If they haven't scared her away by now…"

Well, there go plans A, B, and C.

"But I know Daughtry," Alex says to the bouncer, standing to his full fifty-inch frame. "Let me in."

The bouncer, a hulking white man wearing a cowboy hat that's decorated with what's either mud or maybe blood, shrugs. "No kids in the club."

"Maybe you could call Daughtry and ask," I say, my hand on Alex's shoulder.

"It's against policy." The bouncer leans around me and Alex and checks the IDs of two young women behind us, whose skirts are so short, I wonder if I need to discuss anatomy with my son.

That is not on the agenda for today.

"I understand policy, but this is a matter of love," Alex says. Damn, the kid has balls. Didn't inherit them from me. I make a mental note to thank Josie the next time she calls. "Have you ever been in love?"

The bouncer rolls his eyes, colorless in the neon lights reflected from the glass. "It's a bar. We don't do love here, kid. Only bad decisions."

Alex's face erupts with outrage. "But the Vendetta play here! They don't make bad decisions. The Vendetta is not just about music, they're—"

"Hey, Alex." Selene Huynh, the drummer for the Vendetta, walks past the bouncer, flashing her ID. "What are you doing here?"

"My dad's here to tell Daughtry he loves her," Alex says.

I rub the back of my neck. "Way to make me not sound like a stalker, Alex."

"Thank the goddesses," Selene replies. "She's been miserable since we left Wisconsin. Come on in. Barns, let us through."

Barns the bouncer grumbles and mostly keeps his opinions to himself as Alex and I pass him.

"Thank you," I say, moving quickly to follow in Selene's footsteps. It's challenging, balancing the luggage in one hand and guiding Alex with the other. What kind of parent brings his nine-year-old to a crowded Nashville bar? The entire place smells like stale beer and spilled whiskey.

"Why is the floor sticky?" Alex says, not bothering to lower his voice. It's a good thing, because I wouldn't have been able to hear him in the quiet din of the busy bar.

"Don't ask. And never tell your mother about this."

"I don't think she'll care. We went to this pub in London when I visited her last year. This place smells better. I don't like mushy peas."

Parental pride blossoms in my chest. It mingles with the anxiety over seeing Daughtry, so all I end up with is an acidic, nauseous sensation.

Knocking her drumsticks together, Selene leads us to an empty two-top with a small sign on it saying *reserved*. "We leave it in case family shows. And here you are. Enjoy." She winks at Alex. "I won't tell Daughtry. This is the best kind of surprise."

Alex perches on his stool, while I collapse against mine. The adrenaline from the day has left me feeling woozy. Hopefully I haven't gotten sick from the plane ride.

"Can I get a ginger ale?" Alex asks me, looking through the menu on the table.

A waitress in skin-tight jeans and a halter midi top approaches, and I order Alex's soda and a coffee for me.

"Want a free whiskey back, darlin'?" Her twang reminds me we're no longer in Wisconsin. "We've got a good local one."

"I'm all right. Thank you," I reply. I don't need a hangover on top of whatever the hell it is I'm feeling right now.

Alex's feet bounce against the metal rods of the stool. I open my mouth to tell him to keep still, and act like a respectable person who was not raised in a carnival, but the house lights dim, and the emcee, a short and thin dark brown-skinned man steps to the microphone. He has on a bright red shirt that looks like snakeskin.

"Evening, all! We have quite the lineup for you tonight. Remember. If you like what you hear, clap loud, cheer, and tip your waitresses. Those ladies work hard. Without any further ado, please welcome…Daughtry!"

My heart drops onto the floor, to be trampled by muddy cowboy boots and covered in peanut shells.

Daughtry steps on stage, looking—to put it mildly—fucking amazing. She wears a white and silver A-line dress that flares over her hips, the bodice clinging to the curves of her breasts. All it makes me think of was that little jeweled barbell on her right nipple. What if she's pierced the other one in the last few weeks?

"Good evening, everyone!" Daughtry says, her voice a little too bright. "So happy to vibe with you tonight."

My cock throbs in my pants, like she's its North Star.

"She looks great. Right, Dad?" Alex asks. The waitress drops off our drinks.

I say something along the lines of "Mbleiddiddypopcorn."

Alex simply laughs and sips his ginger ale.

Unsure what to do with my hands—because I can't jerk off in front of everyone in the bar, no matter how badly I want to at that moment—I go for the coffee cup. It's too hot, and scalds my palms.

"Ow fuck," I say, biting off the scream before I draw attention to myself. "Alex, I didn't say that."

"Uh huh," he replies, unconvinced.

Unfortunately, my little outburst is louder than I anticipated, because when I look up at the stage, Daughtry stares right back at me.

CHAPTER 22

 *aughtry*

DECLAN IS HERE? Actually here?

Not some figment of my imagination. No. Alex is with him. There's no way I would have hallucinated him with his kid. I've pictured Declan by himself plenty of times over the last few weeks. Mostly shirtless because holy hell, the man is gorgeous shirtless.

Now, he wears a faded navy blue T-shirt that says *be the solution, not the precipitate* in chipped white letters. Damn it, he looks good. Masculine and lanky and sexy. His hair is disheveled and his cheeks scruffy, like maybe he's been too depressed to shave.

Not unlike my legs. Why the fuck did I stop shaving my legs? It seems of the greatest importance at this exact moment.

Declan glances around nervously, but Alex rescues him.

"Woohoo!" Alex stands up on his chair and starts applauding. "Go, Daughtry! Sing 'Counterfeit'!"

That amazing kid. I startle back into myself and let the grin slide across my face. "We've got fans here tonight, folks! All right, we've gotta listen to the children, right?"

I break into "Counterfeit," then slide seamlessly into "God of Sheep" and "Blue Flannel." This is so much easier than my set in Chicago. I'm vibing better with this crowd, too.

I can't believe they're here. No one has ever gone out of their way to reconnect with me, especially once I ghosted them. I've been sitting backstage, staring at my phone, trying to conjure the words to say to him, but he's *right here*.

It's thrilling and wonderful and my skin feels like it's glowing.

Louise is standing backstage, and if she notices anything about my composure, she doesn't say anything. Good.

Earlier today I called my mom and told her she was cut off. She was pissed—surprise, surprise— but I clearly delineated my boundaries and told her that if she wasn't going to follow them, I wasn't going to answer any more. I started tonight feeling like I was drowning, but now Declan is here and I've resurfaced.

I pretend I'm one hundred percent fine for the whole of my thirty-minute set. I pretend I haven't felt my heart pound for the first time in weeks. I pretend the man I've been dreaming of, day in and day out, isn't sitting ten feet from the stage, staring up at me. Like he missed me, too. Like he hasn't forgotten what he said that night in the tasting room.

Like we have a second chance.

After the applause to my penultimate song, "Kitty Cat Rocks Back," dies down, I find his gaze and hold it. I can't see the color of his eyes with the spotlight on me, but I picture the reassuring cool cyan. This is my chance. I'm about to prove that I'm nothing at all like my mother. I choose to live a different life.

"People say love is all about chemistry," I say into the microphone. Someone in the back of the room groans. "Hey, I would have felt the same, if I hadn't had a good tutor in high school. I was lucky. I had Declan. He taught me everything. All about bonds and reactions and activations. Maybe love is chemistry, but I say that love is like pancakes on a cold winter's day. This song is for Declan Foster. We met when I was eighteen, but it wasn't the right time for us back then. It is, now. I've made a lot of mistakes in my life. But falling in love with him isn't one of them. Falling in love with Declan is…it's like…" It feels right, correct, to say these words to him. My mom falls in lust, in need, in desperation, but never in love.

The entire club is silent, rapt. There's a table of three women near the front, and each of them has tears glistening on their cheeks.

I swallow, the sound reverberating in the mic. "Falling in love is terrifying. I ran away from those feelings because I was scared."

"Whew, feel that, girl!" Someone calls from the back of the club. Maybe the same person with tepid feelings toward chemistry.

The audience titters, but I still gaze at Declan and Alex. "But I'm not scared. Because I have you. I have *people* now. People I care about. People I want to change for, to be better for. Falling in love with Declan isn't a destination. It's a journey. It's the feeling you get when you finally go back to the one place that feels like home."

Alex punches Declan in the arm. He startles for a moment, and then he stands, hands in the pocket of his jeans. "I'm in if you are, Daughtry." His voice is low, gruff, and it sends shivers of liquid pleasure swirling in my core.

"I have to finish my set first," I say, the weight of my guitar heavy in my hands.

"Kiss her!" Someone else calls from the side of the club. This is joined by more and more people, all chanting "Kiss her! Kiss her!"

With sure steps, Declan leaps onstage. He looks like heaven in his punny T-shirt and those jeans that cling to his ass and thighs like they've been sculpted onto him.

I step into his waiting arms. He slides one hand around my waist, and the other along my jaw. Settling my face against his palm, I purr. I'm home. Finally.

Declan's eyes are dark blue again, a shade of ultramarine and gray that promises me all sorts of naughty things. "I've never been onstage before," he says.

"I'll walk you through it." I lean into him and kiss him, long and deep. When the audience cheers, Declan dips me into a backbend, my knee coming up to rest on his thigh.

I would have stayed there forever, but Louise clears her throat behind us. "I'm happy for you, but can you finish your set now?"

Right. Declan pops me back onto both feet. He looks as flushed and thrilled as I feel.

"We'll be right there, little rockstar," he says, pointing to the table where Alex sits with two glasses filled only with ice. Once again, Alex looks unimpressed.

I adore that kid.

I squeeze Declan's hand once more before he leaps off the stage. People cheer again and pat him on the back as he takes his seat.

"Let's get this show back on the road," I say, though my feet are done with wandering. I have my true North, and they're sitting at a table fifteen feet from me.

Tonight, I play for one table, and one table only.

. . .

AFTER THE SET, while the stage hands prep for the Vendetta, I head straight for Declan's table and into his waiting arms. "I missed you so much," I whisper. I hold on tightly, not willing to let go. "I'm so sorry. I let my mom get the best of me, and I freaked out."

He kisses the top of my head, and I want to swoon. "Did you talk to your mom?"

"Yes." The anxiety clamps around my spine, but having Declan here makes it lessen. "I'm setting boundaries. I'm going to try not to let her ruin or control my life."

"Good." Declan tucks a curl of hair behind my ear. "You deserve to be happy, and to live your own life."

"I shouldn't have left."

"You needed to go. You needed to go so you could come home again. We have time, Daughtry."

"What about Ciaran?" Hindsight reminds me that it was a dick move to get into his brother's car, when I know perfectly well that their relationship is strained.

He cups my face between his palms. "Ciaran isn't here. And you're right. It was twelve years ago. I'm not going to let jealousy get the better of me. We can figure everything out, as long as we're together. You're everything I've ever wanted. I love you so much."

I let those words in, really let them in this time, not through a veil of oxytocin and adrenaline. He loves me. A good man loves me, and wants to be with me. We waited twelve years for this moment, but it doesn't matter. They're going to a blip in the years we will spend together, making new memories, forging a new life.

I kiss him again, and pour all my promises to him through this connection. *I'll stay. I love you. We belong to one another.*

It's everything I need, to feel like I belong.

"Daughtry," Alex says, tapping me on the shoulder. "Does this mean you'll give me guitar lessons?"

EPILOGUE

*D*aughtry—*Two Years Later*

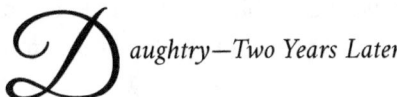

FIFTEEN MINUTES. That's the only window of leeway I have, or this entire plan is going to fall apart.

I've been planning this for the past six months, so *nothing* had better go wrong.

"Calm down, Daughtry." Louise doesn't raise her attention from her phone screen. The plane shudders as it drops in preparation for landing. "We've been over and over the plan. Everything is going to be perfect."

"I know." My tray table convulses when my knee keeps banging into it. I hold my hand over it to settle myself down. "I just don't want to disappoint them."

Louise yawns, and my mouth echoes hers. It's justifiable, after a ten hour flight and amidst a six-month world tour. "Daughtry, Declan thinks the sun rises and sets with you. No one is going to be disappointed, even if you're ten minutes late."

But that's just it. *I* would be disappointed in myself.

I haven't been disappointed in myself since the day I called my mom and told her that she would no longer be getting any money from me, nor would I be speaking to her unless she learned to treat me as a person and not an ATM. It's been two years since we last spoke, and the best two years of my life.

Ever since Declan and I started dating, I committed to make him and Alex a priority. When I tour, we talk every day, multiple times a day. And it never feels like work. It feels like family. Being with them, whether in person or via Skype, fills all the parts of me I haven't realized were empty.

So we make it work.

For someone so buttoned up in public, I haven't expected Declan to be a fan of extravagant gestures. But he's damn good at them.

There was the time I flew back to Wisconsin for a night, simply because I missed him too much to be apart any longer. He was waiting there at the airport for me, with a giant sign, his son, and his parents. They greeted me like I was coming home from war, not a record launch party in New York.

Then there was the time he made a white wine blend for me, the most perfect amalgamation of flavors, and called it One Epic Love Song. It has been winning prizes throughout the Midwest and in some national contests.

Once, I went to Rome, and he ordered my room to be filled with flowers when I arrived. The social media photo of that had gained me four thousand new followers. Most of the comments had read things like *Awwww... Heart eyes... He's a keeper.*

Don't I know that?

I thought we fell in love that weekend two years ago at

the Rock and Wine Festival, but I was wrong. I fall in love with Declan every single day.

The plane lands on the airstrip with a few light bumps, overall a smooth landing, and I check my watch.

I'm right on time.

IT STARTS to rain halfway through the drive from the airport to St. Olaf. It's fine. I planned on that contingency, too.

I park my rental car on one of the side streets, since the parking lot at St. Olaf Elementary is overflowing. Butterflies flit around my stomach, but I don't need to be nervous.

The rain isn't overwhelming, more of a warm June drizzle than a full-out storm. With my umbrella open and earning me several nods of appreciation, I follow the crowds toward the auditorium.

The room is packed with parents, grandparents, siblings, and friends, all dressed in their best rain gear. Several people hold flowers or other gifts, and there's a general party-like atmosphere. Over the stage there is an enormous banner that reads *Congratulations Class of 2024.*

My skin buzzes with anticipation. I made it, and with time to spare.

"Daughtry?"

I whirl around, only to see Zoey and Charlie Foster standing before me. Before I can greet them, Zoey wraps me in her arms.

"Oh, hon, I'm so glad you're here. We didn't think you could make it." Her tears wet the collar of my white and blue raincoat.

"I wanted to surprise them," I say. I kiss Zoey's cheek.

She pulls away and squeezes my hand. "This is wonderful. Alex and Declan are going to be thrilled." With a grin, she tugs at the purple streaks in my dyed-black hair. "This looks good on you."

"Hi, Daughtry." From behind Charlie, Alex's mom Josie waves shyly. I wave back. We've met several times, and have become friends over the last couple years. When we're both in the same place, we make an effort to hang out. She's fun and smart and dedicated, and loves that I make Declan and Alex happy.

"How's the documentary going?" I ask.

"It's going pretty well." Josie is taller than I am, and wearing bright green rain boots and a short-sleeved heather gray knit dress. She has the same blond hair as Alex. How I ever mistook Alex for Ciaran's son, I will never know. His personality is a perfect mix of Josie and Declan. "I'm in Chicago now, editing. I'll send you some scenes, if you want."

"That would be awesome."As much as I like Josie and Zoey, my feet itch to see someone else. I flew literally around the world to see them.

I glance around the assembly. "Where is—"

"Daughtry." Strong arms lift me from behind, and the heady, perfect scent of Declan fills me, from the top of my scalp, all the way to my toes. Declan is an excellent hugger. He spins me toward him, cradling my lower back, and kisses me gently. "I didn't think you'd come."

"I couldn't miss this. It's Alex's fifth grade graduation." I kiss him again, because there is never enough Declan in my life. I love the scratch of the five o'clock shadow he never fully shaves. I love cataloging his moods by the color of his eyes. I love…well, everything about this man.

"Then come on, we don't want to lose our seats." Declan tucks me under his arm and leads me to a row of folding chairs, saved with a mismatched assortment of umbrellas and raincoats. When we sit down, Declan on one side of me, Zoey on the other, then Charlie, Ciaran, and Josie next to her, Declan wraps his around my shoulders and kissed me again. "Thank you. Really. I didn't expect you."

Declan and Ciaran have also slowly repaired their relationship over the past few years.

"The last time I talked to Alex, he looked so disappointed, even though he didn't say anything. So I moved some things around." I unlatch the buttons on my raincoat, revealing my custom T-shirt. Declan takes one look at it and snorts.

"What is that?" He says, pointing toward my breasts.

"My shirt?" I gesture down my chest, at the T-shirt that I had screenprinted with Alex's fifth grade portrait and the words *Alex Rocks* printed across it in neon teal. "It's called a grand gesture."

Declan leans back in his chair, chuckling. "You don't need to woo my kid, Daughtry. He already adores you."

"Then you probably don't want to see the matching umbrella."

Declan laughs louder this time, earning us some bemused stares from our neighbors.

Zoey leans across me to tap Declan on the knee. "Are you going to ask her to marry you after this? Because seriously, what are you waiting for?"

Joy balloons inside me as Declan squeezes me close to him, lining me up against his side. One thing I've learned over the last two years is that Declan is a world-class snuggler. His spooning is Olympic-level dedication. I had to buy a special pillow to mimic the feeling of him beside me in bed for when I'm on the road.

"I'm getting to it," Declan tells his mother. "Don't rush me."

Zoey shrugs and bumps my hip with hers. "This is an amazing gesture, Daughtry."

"Family goes the extra mile for one another," I say.

"Literally." Declan kisses the top of my head as the lights

dim and the middle school orchestra starts playing an off-key "Pomp and Circumstance." "Weren't you in Tokyo? You must be exhausted."

"Nope," I reply, wrapping my arms around him like he's the guidepost I've been looking for all along. "I'm wide awake."

When Alex walks across that stage, the Fosters and I all leap to our feet, whooping and hollering. Honestly, we do that for pretty much every kid in the fifth grade class, because everyone deserves applause on such a momentous day. Alex's eyes widen and his grin nearly splits his face when he sees us.

I'm a part of this. A part of this occasion, and a part of this family. Declan has given me the world in this tiny corner of Wisconsin. Later tonight, I'm going to show him exactly how much he and this family means to me. This is my epic love song.

WANT MORE SMALL TOWN ST. Olaf romance? Curvy baker Laura Marshall meets her grumpy new neighbor love interest in *Sweet and Salty* . There's only one problem. He's in Witness Protection, and his past is barreling toward their future.

For more steamy rockstar romances, check out the rest of the Wine and Rock-n-Roll Series.

Want a free steamy romance? Join my newsletter by clicking here or on the QR code below, and get a completely free, exclusive book!

ABOUT THE AUTHOR

Natalie Cross likes her books like she likes her tea: hot and steamy. Even more so when there are diverse characters who make her laugh, adrenaline to keep her blood pumping, and side characters that steal the show.

Ms. Cross lives in Los Angeles with her family and adorable rescue pup, who refuses to believe his mom has to write instead of taking them for a walk.

For more information, please see her website: www.natal iecrosswrites.com